THE FLEETWOOD CORRESPONDENCE

THE FLEETWOOD CORRESPONDENCE

A Devilish Tale of Temptation

by William Griffin

WIPF & STOCK · Eugene, Oregon

Published by DOUBLEDAY, a division of Bantam Doubleday Dell Publishing Group, Inc., 666 Fifth Avenue, New York, New York 10103

DOUBLEDAY and the portrayal of an anchor with a dolphin are trademarks of Doubleday, a division of Bantam Doubleday Dell Publishing Group, Inc.

Wipf and Stock Publishers
199 W 8th Ave, Suite 3
Eugene, OR 97401

The Fleetwood Correspondence
A Devilish Tale of Temptation
By Griffin, William

ISBN 13: 978-1-55635-800-5
Publication date 1/15/2008
Previously published by Doubleday, 1989

to

E M I L I E

most tempting

PREFACE

I thought that when I had finished researching, indexing, and proofing my biography of C. S. Lewis, I would be through with the Oxbridge professor of literature forever. Instead, when *C. S. Lewis: A Dramatic Life* was within weeks of publication, and as the fruits of my research continued to trickle in, there fell into my hands a manuscript of unusual character.

It looked at first like a sequel to *The Screwtape Letters,* but of course it wasn't, Lewis having written no sequel except "Screwtape Proposes a Toast," a fragment that appeared in *The Saturday Evening Post,* December 19, 1959.

A closer look at the manuscript revealed a number of substantial differences between the manu-

. . . .

script of Lewis's epistolary novel, which at the present time is in the Berg Collection at the New York Public Library, and the manuscript of what I am calling, quite arbitrarily, *The Fleetwood Correspondence.*

Lewis wrote *Screwtape* in ink, his nib dipped into a well, his scrawl running from edge to edge of the onionskin stationery, leaving no space for margins. The author of *Fleetwood,* on the other hand, seems to have composed on a word processor and produced the text, by virtue of a letter-quality, daisy wheel printer, on twenty-pound bond paper; there are airy margins and, the manuscript having been burst and collated, microperforations on all four sides of the paper.

The typescript reads as though it might have been written by Lewis himself; it couldn't, internal evidence revealing that *Screwtape* had been composed during the Second World War; the young man who was Wormwood's target, you will remember, was killed by an intracontinental rocket. *Fleetwood,* on the other hand, seems surely to have been written in the age of the intercontinental missile. The locale of the former is London; of the latter, New York, where Lewis never visited. And, of course, the spelling in the one is British; in the other, American.

Differences apart, the two works have a remarkable resemblance. They both affirm that there is

. . . .

a Devil, that this creature has other such creatures who are subservient, that they have personalities, that they have definite assignments on this earth, that sometimes they succeed, sometimes they fail. And, of course, they are both works of fiction, not directories of spiritual guidance. Whatever other resemblances and differences the two works have, I leave to the reader.

Please note that the identities of both the writer and the recipient of the letters that follow are unknown. Since "Uncle" and "Nephew" are notorious as code names in diabolic correspondence, and although some of the characters—I don't know how else to describe them—seem to have names, I have not attempted to identify them further.

Please note also that the letters as I found them had no dates. I have had to arrange them in what seems a chronological order; the liturgical year helps, the first letters being written before Advent, the last ones at the end of Lent; those that I have not been able to place in this manner, I have inserted where they seem thematically comfortable. The ordering of all the letters, as indicated by the Roman numeral preceding each letter, is mine.

William Griffin
September 29, 1988
Feast of the Archangels

THE FLEETWOOD CORRESPONDENCE

I

Most fetid Uncle,

What the devil are you doing at Dimchurch?

I just found your address in the *Directoire Internationale Diabolique,* in the red pages no less!

The reason I am writing to you is that riffling through my files the other day, I came across a packet of letters from your filthiness. You must have written them—was it forty-five years ago?—when you sent me to London on my first assignment.

Reading them now reminded me how painfully cruel you were when we were novices and you were novice master, teaching us how to lure sheep from the fold and shepherd them to Hell.

How I detested writing those weekly reports! I

. . . .

was failing miserably. Everything I did was wrong. Nothing seemed to work as the soul assigned to me—the patient as you called him—glided so gracefully from darkness to light.

How I dreaded the arrival of your letters each week, full of correspondence-course chitchat—"a major Arsenius is much to be preferred to a minor Arsenius"—that read so cleverly but had no practical use. And your spiteful comments on my writing style sent me into deep despair.

Let it be said once and for all—and I don't mind being the one to say it—that my writing style was, is now, and ever shall be a thousand times more suave, more suasive than yours!

Why your letters were so unhelpful, so hateful, escaped me at the time. But now, forty-five years later, I can see that you wanted us to fail. Those who cannot tempt, teach, and those who teach, cannot tolerate success in those they have taught.

I knew my assignment in London was meant to test me, one of the Infernal Prince's seven great experiments for tyros. And it did not take a revelation to know there was no way I could fail . . . as indeed there was no way I could succeed. If I bagged the soul, it would not be the less painful for me; and if the soul managed to get away, it would not be the more painful.

. . . .

But when the soul in quest had sailed—spinnakers ahoy—into that far-off port, I knew you would erupt. I knew you meant to extinguish me, throw me into outer darkness, toss me—zissssh—like a torch into the moat.

Well, I got the hell out, as the colloquialism so aptly puts it, took the flame with me, and flew until I found a new territory, "terra incognita" on your tattered novitiate map, but "America" on the relief map in my glass-walled office.

Strolling about the forest floors and concrete canyons, the carpety lawns and wheaty fields of this massive new continent were angelic creatures. Like me, they were the castoffs of older, arrogant societies, occidental and oriental cities, pocked with excess, powdery with rot. Immediately, in this postlapsarian paradise, with delightful derelicts on all sides, I felt at home.

So populous is this country that I do not, as you did, have the luxury of stalking one soul at a time. If I wanted to make a dent, I would have to divide the tens of millions into significant populations according to want or desire, then develop specific strategies for each. I have established a number of divisions like Commandments and Capital Sins. Each division has a number of strategy managers. Each strategy manager has a productivity goal, which is, in

. . . .

its simplest form, a share of the market larger than both last year's and the competition's.

I use memory bubbles, disclosing wafers, and other products of the new technologies. I apply the Heideggerian notion of entrapment, the Bultmannian theory of increasing distinctness, and other gewgaws of the new scholarship. I manipulate the Harvard scale of susceptibility, the Stanford ell of implausibility, and other modes of collegial measurement. I have blended mental disease and spiritual fatigue into a disappearing crème. I have induced a television evangelist, haranguing his audience on self-denial, to overdose on divinity fudge. And the Bible, that vile volume, now appears in an edition with diabolical references devotionally capitalized and rubrically printed.

Ahhh, yes, America the temptable was a paradise before 1942, all Adams and Eves bronzing their skins in the sun. Striding about, I felt like a missionary hungry for converts, with what seemed "Choice of Aborigine" for lunch. But since my arrival in the Northern Hemisphere, it has been a run for the fig leaves, a rush for the shrubbery. The only thing naked in public these days is I . . . and then only on special feasts and ferials when I choose to display my infernality for admiration and adoration.

I must end this epistle now if I expect to get it

. . . .

into the European pouch. Discorde—I did not defect alone—now travels at four and one half times the speed of virtue. The only sound heard in the cabin as she passes through the barrier is the tinkling of virginity shattered.

Write if you want to, but I expect no answer.

Yours triumphantly,

Fleetwood

II

Most loathsome Uncle,

I would not be writing to you so soon again if Carcinoma had not brought me the news. You are indeed in Dimchurch, she tells me, and in a senior denizens' home. She found you huddled before the hearth, a mere ember of your former self.

You showed no signs of recognition when she read my letter to you, or so she said. She thought that was due to old age. I hastened to explain to her that you never showed me recognition even when you were young. That is to say, except when you sent me those silly letters while I was in London. Why was it, I wonder, that after I was sent down from *Schola*

. . . .

Temptorum you could communicate with me only by letter, never face to face?

Before you fall from ember to ash, I send you this missive about the state of Christianity in America. I hesitate to tell you about it for fear that it will make you feel the better, but I will tell it to you anyway, trumpeting my successes, knowing that it will make you feel the worse.

Christianity is wildly successful in America, flowering everywhere. Each Christian is convinced of the correctness of his or her species and indeed of the speciousness of all others. One classifies another as *flora non grata,* only to be labeled in return as *herba inutilis.*

All the while, of course, infiltrating their ranks, are undercover agents Wilt, Rust, Mildew, Leafspot, and Damping-Off. (The names are metaphorical, of course; I would not reveal their real identities even to you!) Not so subtle are my mechanized divisions under Aphid, Borer, Mite, Miner, and Thrip.

If for one moment all the florific species could turn their attention from themselves and concentrate their fury on me, I'd be trapped like a fly on an insectivorous perennial. But of course, these Christians, lovely flowering creatures that they are, have no eyes for me. They merely follow the sun, while I

. . . .

carry on my program of progressive floricide. Soon the field—much of it already in rubble and stubble—will be entirely mine.

Let me change the metaphor from plants to pastry, which may make you gag, but Christianity, as you served it up in the novitiate—lumpy, goiterous pudding—never did help my digestion.

Ask me what Christianity is, and I will tell you that it is a pie, that Christian communions are slices of the pie, and that membership is indicated by the size of the slices. Ask a Christian what he is, and he will tell you what slice he belongs to, not that he is a lemon meringue or she a lemon chiffon. Rarely can he recite his creed, if he has one. More rarely can she tell you what the articles of that creed mean, if indeed they have any meaning.

Some Christians think that there is a saving grace in membership; being in the pie is what counts. Other Christians think that being in the pie is not enough; one must reside in the right slice so that when the heavenly hunger calls, they will tastefully enter the divine digestion. Membership, if only those huckleberries knew it, is not salvation; it is mere salivation, and I will not be satisfied until I, not He, have slurpily devoured every slice.

Yes, Christianity is a circle, but it's not the wedges that count; it's the concentric circles emanat-

. . . .

ing from the center. The innermost circle, the one that cuts across all slices, is orthodoxy. In it reside, in greatest concentration, Christians from all communions who hold most dear—and indeed for dear life—the core of Christian doctrine. And it is on orthodoxy's eye that I have taken deadly aim.

Time passes so quickly when one is succeeding. In this letter, I have merely presented the pie, sliced it, and served it. In my next letter, I shall tuck my napkin in place and eat it, all of it, right in front of my minicam, and shall send you the videotape. Merciful creature that I am, I shall enclose the pie knife for your licking.

Defiantly yours,

Fleetwood

III

Most rancid Uncle,

Especially stinging was the remark, reported to me by Carcinoma through Discorde, that tempting millions was mere melodrama, that I could never tempt successfully just one individual. To prove you woefully wrong, I shall, more for my own amusement than for your edification, attempt a single individual . . . and this in my spare time. Such has been my success in the New World that I do not have to work the weekends.

I have already picked that person out, one superior in all respects to the ridiculously weak one you assigned me decades ago. He would eventually have fallen to my blandishments, you very well know, if

. . . .

the rocket hadn't fallen on him betimes, blowing to bloody bits both his past and my future.

First, the temptand is a woman, which means that her actions under pressure will surely titillate the crowd. You would use the word "intuitive" to describe that sex's reactions to anything serious. You would define the feminine sex as "not inferior" or "not unequal" ; I would define it rather as "equal and perhaps superior." Her sex I take far more seriously than you would have, and by virtue of my superior coordination, I am able to match her unpremeditated zigs with some unpredictable zags of my own.

Second, the temptand is young, not many years out of college. Like a milliner's creation she wears the fashionable idea that she should not follow the traditional path of women in her family and indeed in the history of humankind. She has decided not to marry, conceive, rear children, and sustain a husband—at least right now. Rather, she has decided to leave the relatively quiet, sweet-smelling parishes of a southern state for the noisy, sleepless precincts of a northern metropolis, where she hopes to earn her fame and fortune.

Third, she has no particular religion, although she shows marked attraction to the glittering articles found in a church gift shop. She has been brought up in a denomination that pretends to be Christian but

. . . .

has few creedal pretensions. But what is important here is that she has not been baptized in any important way; that is to say, she has not been immersed or sprinkled; she has not even expressed a desire for that watery rite.

Fourth, she is well educated in the manner not unknown at English universities. But her education presents no unscalable barrier to temptation. Knowledge has never been virtue, although philosophers fumble to prove it so. If I were to select three volumes from her bookshelf that would reveal the sort of soul she has, I would pick out *The Bible Designed to Be Read as Literature* (dust kittens on the gilt edges), *The Effective Executive* (coffee rings on the dust jacket), and *The Joy of Cooking* (thready stubs where the red ribbons used to be).

The fact that she is well read, however, means that she is a prime candidate for that sort of higgledy-piggledy conversion process whereby the convertend reads what converts before her have written, thus perceiving a road paved with pages of argument and exhortation, cobbles leading, it would seem, into the new Jerusalem.

Well, the road into Jerusalem is also the road out of Jerusalem, as more than one spiritual writer has pointed out, and I shall lead our tasty young temptand, the conversion volumes pressed to her

. . . .

bouncing breasts, from our Enemy's holy city right down the Adamized interstate to our own holy city of Gehenna.

Never have you, the much-vaunted tempter of tempters, approached such a splendid creature. Nowhere in your sordid, ill-organized training manual have you developed strategies for containing such a voluptuous personage. Hence, I have had to invent my own, and such is my confidence that I shall allow her every freedom to resist. Such is my ingenuity, my artistry, that I cannot but achieve success.

The dangerous game is afoot, and I shall tell you of my progress as it happens. Have no fear that I will not tell you the truth. I have no need to lie. Truth is as much ours as theirs.

With this missive I am sending you some Gatorade. It restores in one orifice what you are losing so rapidly from another.

Spitefully yours,

Fleetwood

IV

Most fractious Uncle,

You used to gloat that you led your patient out of the reading room at the British Museum, suggesting that it was better for him to eat lunch than to follow a line of reasoning that might eventually put him onto the primrose pathway to the infernal votive flame.

I, on the other hand, to show my superiority to you, led this young woman, at the very hour of lunch, right to New York Public Library Central, past the eroding lions, up the marble steps into the lobby, and up the curling staircase to the second and third floors.

I even let her pause for a moment in front of

. . . .

an atrocious tapestry hanging on the wall and let her contemplate the woven scene, two Dominicans—"watchdogs of the Lord," they call themselves—scrivening at their *scrinia,* copying the literary past for the illiterate future, while outside their very window war rages on.

That was what she was looking at, but that was not what she saw. To counteract this inaccurate and indeed unjust portrayal of human history, I had taken the trouble to place over the hoary rag a transparency that depicts in the foreground the hellish war between the forces of good and evil and in the background the two monks looking out the window, recording for posterity the triumph of evil over good.

She sniffed at it, the temptand did, and took no note of it, alas, her liberal education never having included art appreciation. Then she entered the public catalog room wherein are housed thousands of trays of index cards, darting like splintery tongues from wooden cases. So old is the wood and so humid the environment that the varnish sticks to the fingers of the person immersed in research.

These she passed by, knowing apparently the whereabouts of what she was looking for, veering right into the main reading room, south. Past the long oaken tables, the heavy curved-back chairs sitting

. . . .

like sentinels around them, and made her way to a ladder that took her up to the gallery.

There she confronted hundreds of similarly bound volumes, a series, Migne's *Patrologia Latina.* When she came to Volume XLVIII, she pulled it out and found in it, without much difficulty, the Christmas sermons of Augustine and settled down to read the rippling rhetoric of the bishop of Hippo, whose lustful itch once put him within moments of our grasp.

Her reading, however, did not have the effect that I intended. Believe it or not, she liked the Latin. Indeed, she was dazzled by the metaphors—it reminded her of fireworks on the Mississippi on New Year's Eve—and from that deduced the vitality of his devotion. When her lunch hour was over, she slid the volume back onto the shelf, climbed down from the gallery, descended the stairs, and walked out into the early afternoon sun, all the while wondering if what the gospels said took place on that first Christmas Day did indeed take place and wondering further if what Augustine wrote in a full-blown fashion some three hundred years later was really true.

She has not yet found a job in the big city. She went to yet another employment agency, insisting that she was a writer and that she wanted a job in advertising. The agent sized her up, trying to find out just how far she would go, how much she would pay for a job, and whether it was worth his while to sleep with her. He made some telephone calls and set up some interviews.

The interviewers were mostly young men who would as soon try her virtue as tend to her job application. Those that were not young men were middle-aged women, who were looking for protégées or female companionship more of a sexual than a professional kind.

She will fall and fall many times before I am through with her—scuffing her shoes, bruising her palms, running her stockings—and I will prevent her from rising too quickly. She is no nearer to baptism now than she was when I met her.

So the lemon-flavored Gatorade didn't agree with you. I'm sending you the orange-flavored. Carcinoma tells me that your prognosis is not good, that senility has sapped your sinews, and that it is only a matter of time before your glowing coals glow no more. To make these last few moments as painful as possible, I shall continue reporting on my temptand, who will fall, I do not hesitate to predict, like a stainless-steel luge down an infinite slope.

Ingratiatingly yours,

Fleetwood

V

Most cankerous Uncle,

What do you mean, where did I get my temptand? The same place you got yours. From an Opposite Number, the very existence of whose species you kept from us at *Schola Temptorum.* Why is it that none of us undergraduates was ever told that an Opposite Number would be assigned to us throughout our temptorial career, that we would never be unaccompanied wherever we would go, and that for every move we would make, our Opposite Number would make a separate but equal countermove?

My only conclusion is that you knew part of the story but not all of it, and that you yourself had not risen high enough up the executive ladder to

. . . .

achieve this confidential knowledge. Another theory —advanced by Jester or Fester, I can't recall which twin it came from—was that it was yet another example of your twisted sense of humor, like handing a lighted firework to a child and waiting for it to explode and blow the poor tot's hand off.

If you must know, after getting your letter of challenge, I immediately requested an interview with my Opposite Number. I telephoned him; after several rings his answering machine was activated, telling me, in lyrics composed to go with "Angels We Have Heard on High," that he was not able to come to the phone at this time but that if I left my number and a message, he would return the call.

Well, I left my number but not my message and said that it was an emergency. That was Monday. Tuesday I called five times; each time I got the answering machine. By Wednesday I was shouting blasphemies and obscenities into the instrument. Still no return call. By Thursday I had given up the idea, and by Friday I had forgotten about it.

On Saturday I was sleeping rather later than usual, after a particularly strenuous week, when my subterrancan suite was invaded; I was bundled in blankets, dragged up the marble stairs, shoved rudely into the back of a vehicle, and carted most cruelly to an abandoned garage, where I was thoroughly worked

. . . .

over by some angelic goons in polyester suits and severely admonished by Opposite Number, who, by the way, was wearing a silk suit from Sulka's, for not leaving a message when I called.

I could have insulted him; indeed, I'm sorry I didn't. Instead, I got right to the point. I wanted a temptand, and I wanted one fast. He seemed aware of the temptorial challenge emanating feebly from Dimchurch. He laughed at me, said I would fail as dismally as I had the first time, but that he would go along with the joke for his own amusement. He doffed his Dobbs and asked me to reach into it. He held the hat above eye level, and I supposed that it contained the names and addresses of thousands of temptands in the metropolitan New York area. There was only one slip of paper in the hat, however, and it took almost a minute—what with the way he jiggled it back and forth—to get my fingers firmly on it. When I asked why there was only one, he said he wanted to give me a fighting chance. I had a hundred other questions, but he and his herald angels got into the longest limousine I think I have ever seen and roared off, diesel fumes choking my rented lungs. One would think that an archangel of his stature would be able to control the pollution in his exhaust!

Now you know how I came by my temptand, and now you will see, if your weeping eyes will allow

. . . .

you to read my missives, how I shall wrest her from the Supernal Kingdom's grasp.

Yours titillatingly,

Fleetwood

VI

Most captious Uncle,

No, this is no ordinary temptand, and yes, she does read Latin. Such is her fluency in that vulgar tongue that she has perused Virgil's national epic, the love poems of Catullus, and the science fiction of Lucretius, the Asimov if not the azimuth of the classical world. But never in her education at preparatory school or college had she encountered what her teachers sneeringly referred to as Church Latin. And if I had my way, she would never have found the Fathers of the Church. But for the misfortunate circumstance of meeting a young man who knew about them, she would be still in the dark.

"Unprepossessing" is a word that overly describes the red-haired creature in green corduroy, leather-buttoned jacket. "His flashing eyes, his floating hair," he looks as though he stepped right out of the pages of "Kubla Khan." He was drawn to her in the first place because she liked to read books and to talk about books. On his first visit to her tiny brownstone apartment, he was surprised and delighted to find on the shelf such revealing volumes as the poems of Emily Dickinson, a biography of Sarah the first duchess of Marlborough, to whom she was somehow related, and *Southern Cooking* by Mrs. S. R. Dull, which she was trying to master.

This young man, who reminds me of nothing so much as an Irish setter, is a well-churched person in the Roman fashion, one of those who from childhood seems to have made a pact with the Supernal Lord. For a time, modeling himself on the Lone Ranger, a masked man of pretentious symbology, he had even taken steps toward becoming a clergyperson. After eight years, low marks if not low self-esteem sent him back to the world, where now he seems destined to do my cause some real harm. Not like so many others, though, who when they abandoned their clerical career, left behind their theological baggage, this simple creature brought his carpetbag with him and is dazzling the temptand with all sorts of doctrinal trinkets.

. . . .

Cooking a southern meal for him one night, she explained her "theodyssey," her need to abandon the denomination she was brought up in and to seek somewhere meaningful to go on Sundays. She told how she had gone back to the library to read more of Augustine's sermons. (It was the Irish setter, hereinafter referred to as Fido, who had led her there in the first place, having barely made her acquaintance and answering almost her first question.)

But she was confused. Should she read the Bible? Should she read more of the early Christian writings? Should she join a biblical church or a liturgical church? Although he was an unshakable member of his own communion, Fido did not try to recruit her, even though I urged him to aggravate her in this regard. She had begun a pilgrimage, he had the banality to say, and it didn't seem to matter which church lay at the end, just so long as she took further steps along the way. Then he mumbled something about the Third Person of the Supernal Trinity's having a hand in all of this—at which point I exercised one of my few infernal prerogatives: I tipped the steaming platter of red beans and rice right into his lap.

Sportively yours,

Fleetwood

VII

Most catastrophic Uncle,

You asked me where my temptand came from. Well, her dossier mailed to me by Opposite Number—it took four weeks to travel forty city blocks—has finally arrived. A surprisingly thick one, it reveals that, not many months before, she had suffered a stunning moral reversal in a rain forest on one of those islands off the coast of Florida. She had not suspected her own fragility, and so when her image of herself was shattered like a champagne glass against a chimney brick, it brought her face to face with reality and dropped her to her knees, grumbling and mumbling all manner of Goddlebygook [*sic*].

Looking back at what she had done was too

. . . .

painful, she thought on the plane trip back to New York. She was overcome, oddly enough, by a sort of nostalgia. It was as though she were only now receiving communications from outer space that had been broadcast to her alone aeons ago. Was there an intelligence out there trying to communicate with her? Was she intelligent enough to know that the intelligence who was trying to get in touch with her was nowhere, neither up nor down, within nor without?

At thirty-seven thousand feet, flying northward along the Atlantic coastline, she tried her damnedest to communicate back. Electronics were of no use, of course, so she closed her eyes, climbing in her imagination up a cliff and signaling what appeared to be a cliff facing her in the distance, wigging and wagging with colorful flags. Once or twice during the two-hour trip, she thought she saw that someone was signaling to her. (I am using metaphor, of course, but then so was she.) On landing at La Guardia, she felt the keenest desire to find, wherever He was hiding, the Supernal Lord.

How these people are able to identify a simple longing with the Supernal Lord is hard for me to understand. It has nothing to do with magnetism or radioactivity or other laws of the physical universe; rather it is a spiritual law whose analog is gravity, a continuous pulling in an attractive direction. I deny

. . . .

this, of course, and say that she, and countless others like her, are victims of imaginations that never stop.

Since she has had this desire, she has increased her highly calorific reading, which was already at the level of one book a day, whether hardcover or paperback. In particular, she has returned to fairy tales and children's stories, to the works of Grimm and Andersen, Potter and Grahame, and found in them and their secret gardens, with egresses to wild and exotic parks and paradises, what appeared to be a path laid down in powdered gold, a track through the woods that she assumed would lead her to the Supernal Lord.

At this discovery she spun about, not knowing whether she wanted to contemplate or to act. The desire she felt was pleasurable in itself, a lingering melody, a sort of lolling about in lingerie, an echo from a tale told long ago; but the past had no lessons, I urged her to conclude, however much she sifted through it.

Then she would go forward, she thought, following the trail of the golden talc, expecting an adventure not found in literary epics or creation myths. But at the end of the track she will find not the Supernal Lord (He's far too busy to remember who she is), and certainly not the Infernal Prince (He doesn't even know she exists), but me, and I will grab her around

. . . .

the middle and slam her to the ground and pummel her until she admits I exist.

It would be churlish, I suppose, not to tell her about the other equal and opposite existence. But that my Opposite Number will certainly do, if he hasn't done it already. It is enough that I confront her with evil rude and simple and convince her that I lurk behind every leaf on the golden pathway of desire.

Weekends should do it, and it should not take many more weeks before she is willingly mine.

Yours efficaciously,

Fleetwood

Most phthisicky Uncle,

My darling young temptand—and I like her for it—is a scrappy twentieth-century pagan who wants to wrestle with the great intellectual arguments for the existence of God. Well, have I arranged a confrontation for her!

The following, by the way, was reported to me by my assistants Sorites and Enthymeme, who swore to stop arguing with each other long enough to attend to the temptand as she participated, as it were, in a series of chess matches with masters from the history of thought.

First was with the master who wanted to prove the existence of God from motion. It was noontime at

. . . .

the accessories counter in a posh department store, where there was a lot of commotion to get the salesperson's attention. The temptand pushed, albeit inadvertently, the woman in front of her. "Watch who you're shoving!" said the glossed and glazed Vreelandic creature. "I'm sorry," said the temptand, "but someone pushed me." "Then tell that person to shove off!" My temptand turned around, but the person behind her was already gone . . . and intuitively she got the picture in her mind of a finite series of people turning around to tell a pusher or shover to stop pushing or shoving until the second-to-last person in the line turned to face the last person, who just happened to be the prime pusher or shover. But would that person be God, I whispered into her ear, and in Bloomingdale's of all places? That was on Monday.

On Tuesday she matched wits with the argument from efficient causality, which came up in a discussion with Fido. What happened when a chalked cue propelled a solid ball over a field of green felt toward a striped one? Efficient causality was like that, an ordered series of balls, each kissing another because it itself had been kissed, leading back to the person who himself held the first cue. He was certainly the unkissed kisser, the first efficient cause. He might even be the billiard champion of the world, but

. . . .

was he God? I asked her. Wasn't he merely one who hustled the idea of God?

On Wednesday she encountered the third proof, which argued from contingency. Once there was nothingness—now there was somethingness. Contingent creatures must have a necessary uncreated creature to explain their being. Of this argumentation she could make neither head nor tail. In its reverse form, however, the argument from something to nothing seemed to explain the proliferation of potholes on the island's pavements.

On Thursday, she confronted the proof from grades of perfection while writing copy for ads that she was putting into her sample book. One detergent was claimed to be superior to others on the ground of a transcendental perfection. But the detergent did not have this perfection in its fullness by its very nature. Hence, it had to derive its perfection from outside, from some absolutely perfect cause that was not only exemplary but also efficient. This argument my temptand was not sure would wash successfully. Indeed, she felt that there was a certain amount of dirt backwash in the argumentation.

On Friday, she received from her parents, by virtue of United Parcel, the archery set with which she had won many a contest at summer camp. Stringing the bow and aiming it at an imaginary butt, she

. . . .

thought that as an arrow was directed toward the concentric circles, so also was the acorn growing unerringly into an oak. As the feathery shaft depended entirely on the archer for its target-seeking flight, so also the nubbly nut depended completely on something outside of itself. Lack of knowledge on the part of arrow and acorn seemed to presuppose that there was someone outside who supplied it. This argument corresponded with her strong perception of the orderly operation of naturc, but, I asked her, inserting the seed of doubt into what I hoped was fertile soil, was the paradisal Robin Hood or the primal plantsman—really God?

At week's end my temptand felt that she had lost all five matches. Indeed, all she could picture in her mind's eye was a wide lapel to which had been affixed a huge white button reading, "I Am the One and Only."

"But how do you know," asked her red-haired friend, extending her metaphor, "that you aren't left with a Grand Central Station full of oddly dressed persons, all of whom are wearing buttons with messages on them like 'First Cause' and 'Prime Mover,' 'Billiards über Alles' and 'Ducks in a Row?'

"You make it sound like a *New Yorker* cartoon. What am I supposed to do next?"

. . . .

"Why not go up to one of them and start talking?"

"But what'll I say?"

"You could ask for directions?"

"What good will that do?"

"Well, once you start talking, the other person will have to answer, and before you know it, you have begun to pray."

"You are out of your mind!"

There is yet another argument, dear Uncle, that I could have foisted on her, and it may turn out to be the best argument yet, moving as it does from annihilation to exnihilation. But I prefer not to philosophize on the weekend; it's the only time I have not to think.

Deductively yours,

Fleetwood

IX

Most noisome Uncle,

One thing my delicious young temptand has done religiously every Sunday morning since her arrival in New York City is buy the *Times*, lug the tendentious, ten-pound parcel back to her apartment, pull out the classified advertisements, and look for a job. What she wanted, poor dear, was employment in film or television or advertising. She could write her way out of a brown paper bag, she felt, and therefore could conquer the world.

No part of Sunday did she really keep holy, thanks to my considerable efforts. She wrote letters to those ads specifying a box number, giving her qualifications, albeit slim, and indicating her salary require-

. . . .

ments, which she felt ought not to be as slender as her experience.

Sunday evening she invited Fido over to her apartment. I was relaxing as they spent the evening talking, not about things divine but rather about survival in the big city. Some amorous adventures of a particularly dull and uninspiring sort prolonged the evening. It concluded, however, not with a pang of pleasure but with the gong of guilt.

I should perhaps have expected it from him, a hyperventilating moralist, but from her, a newcomer to the moral Sargasso, I could never have predicted it. It was as though some navigational instrument deep inside her told her she had entered the calms of Capricorn, where her sails would slack, her cheeks burn, her tongue grow parched, all being punishments for her adventuring on the high spiritual seas.

Her young man is having a bad influence on her—of that there can be no doubt. I shall have to, as quickly as possible, surround her with those who think that prancing about in the bed of one to whom one is not joined conjugally is not only pleasurable but also desirable. So much pain awaits her when she shall have died that I think she should have as much pleasure now as she can hold.

But I had this uneasy feeling that if I were going to succeed with her on weekends, I would have

. . . .

to know what she did during the week. Hence, before retiring for the night, I assigned two of my best to follow her from sunrise Monday to sunset Friday; they were not to act in my behalf, merely to reconnoiter.

When Monday morning arrived in Manhattan, she dressed quickly and walked out onto the sidewalk, shadowed still by tall buildings, the sun jogging up the east-to-west-running streets. She did not notice as she set out that only a step or two behind her were Blister and Glister, hard-driving operatives of mine who were recuperating from a particularly difficult but spectacularly successful assignment with a bishop, who ended dramatically, diving from a tall steeple into a watered-down doctrine the size of a kitchen sponge. It is from their report that I am basing much of this letter.

At the corner eatery where she breakfasted every morning, she ordered the usual. While sitting there, spooning her coffee, waiting for the eggs to be scrambled, the wheat bread to be toasted, she listened distantly to the waistcoated man behind the counter, who was babbling something about this not being his real job, his being an actor and waiting for something to turn up, and—funny thing—about his having been laid by a woman twice his age over the weekend.

When she heard his version of the story, it

. . . .

sounded like Rabelais on Long Island, but when she reflected on her own escapade the night before, it wasn't half so funny. She felt guilty all over again, although she was not sure why. She would ask her red-haired friend when she met him for lunch.

Thus fortified, although she would have given a great deal for a dish of grits with melting butter and syrup, she hit the street again and walked toward the employment agency that had had the largest ad in the Sunday *Times.* Past St. Bartholomew's Episcopal Church she walked, unaware of her malangelic escort, and past St. Patrick's Cathedral, oblivious that our Supernal Enemy was housed there and, indeed, that there actually were humanoids inside the edifice, participating in worshipful acts.

At the agency office, which was a no-nonsense male emporium, she filled out a form, attached her résumé, and waited for an agent to see her, reading back issues of *Ad Age* and *Business Week.* A half hour later, when a man did see her, he said that, first of all, the job market was tight, but that she looked promising. When she asked him point blank how the market could be tight when there were so many ads in the paper, he smiled and said he could make some telephone calls on her behalf.

This scene repeated itself with several variations before the morning was over. By the time she

. . . .

met Fido, she was totally depressed. He, however, seemed filled with helium. He took her by the hand and led her crosstown. She asked him why she felt so bad about last night when what they had done was so good. He said that he too felt bad and that he had promised the Supernal Lord that he would not do it again.

Intentionally, however, they were right. Intentionally, she asked? What does that mean? And then they were in Cartier's. He had acted badly last night, he said, but he had had the noblest of intentions. Now he wanted to give her something. And he bought her, against the severest protestations that he couldn't afford it on his minuscule salary as a contract writer for an assurance society, what she had picked out, a small gold cross, that damnable symbol, and a thin gold chain.

Glister was severely chastised, I hasten to say, for this egregious slip. Of all my personnel—Sequin is her middle name!—she should have been able to make shine more brightly every other metallic thing in the jeweler's display case. Her defense, that she was completely drained from her previous assignment, I refused to accept. There was some truth to what she said, but I could not let her see that. If only there were some vampirical way to rejuvenate her. Cadmium, who labors in research and development,

. . . .

has promised soon some sort of electrical rechargement; I shall have to prod him to accelerate his efforts.

In the afternoon, with Blister close on her heels, pitter-pattering about in her Papagallos, she visited yet another advertising agency. On the way up the elevator in the glass-faced building, the door opened on a floor housing the offices of a cosmetics firm. She thought she saw, before the doors closed, a short, smartly dressed young man hurrying past, leaning as if into the wind, a pillow in his hand, and on the pillow a shapely jar of cream or crème.

At the agency itself, which was on the thirtieth floor, she was confronted by the most ripe of receptionists, whose beauty if not brains qualified her for representing the agency up front. The creative director seemed to like my temptand when he finally got around to seeing her. He suggested that employment involved long hours and sometimes after-hours work. She said that was not disagreeable to her. He said not to call him; he would call her.

Discouraged, she left the agency and walked slowly toward the East River, Blister steering her clear of St. Thomas's Episcopal Church. Like a dancer escorting his partner across a parquet floor for the thousandth time, he closed his eyes and went straight ahead. She, however, peeled off and went

. . . .

into St. Peter's Lutheran Church. Blister was half a block away by the time he noticed that he tangoed by himself.

He quickly retraced his patent-leather steps, but it was too late. She had already prayed that the Supernal One, if indeed there were such a one, would grant her a favor. A job. Blister I had lanced immediately, his overweening pride suppurating all over the sidewalk.

The young devils of today, it would seem, want only a good time; they don't want to work hard; they don't want to achieve goals. I would say that, except that it would make me sound old. But I am not old. You are old, and I only hope that you can hear this letter when Carcinoma spouts it into your ear trumpet.

Vitally yours,

Fleetwood

X

Most crapulous Uncle,

You protest too much about the cross, even as you drank too much when you were young, dribbling the bitter down your chin and neck into your shirt. If you were so concerned about those right-angled rods, you would never have allowed so many of them to have survived the Blitz. Think what an opportunity the follies of human history handed you! Know what a bungle you made of it, churches smashed but not demolished, parachute mines drifting past steeples and into office buildings!

Perhaps your most hideous characteristic—it is not easy to choose just one—is your holding others to a standard that you yourself were never able to

. . . .

meet. I, on the other hand, am a sort of classical hero, in the mold of Hector and Achilles, able to walk in front of my troops and challenge the Supernal Enemy to personal combat, winner take all. At most, you were a mere manager, managing only to hide behind a wall of paper, personal correspondence, interoffice memoranda; a teacher whose chiefest weapons were the classroom pointer and the chalkboard eraser, whose victims were those younger ones entrusted to you for their education.

If the cross as symbol has had the devastating effect in history that you claim, why did the previous generations of devils perform so poorly in front of it? Why, when they had the chance several centuries ago, didn't they incite the reformers, who were wandering about hammering into dust the heads on saintly statuary, to pulverize all the crosses instead? An extravagant waste of energy, it now seems to me.

You have no sense of history, but I have. I know that in this young temptand of mine is all of the history of the struggle between our Infernal Prince and their Supernal Lord, from whom He disgracefully dissented. I know also that if I win this soul for the Infernal Kingdom, I shall have reversed, at least in some small way, the devastating effects of our Infernal Prince's initial dissent, his descent down the icy

. . . .

slope, then off the glass-slicked jump, his matchstick skis snapping like twigs, his limbs flailing about in the frosted air.

Yes, she is now wearing the cross, but her oily skin will soon turn the gold a grimy green. And yes, even before you ask, I know that gold is chemically impervious to sweat. You won't have to write me about that next week. But I shall find some way to tarnish it so that she will never think it anything else than a token of love.

Have you ever noticed how in film—I know you never went to the cinema but you left feeling debauched—I mean, in that species of modern film in which diabolical possession is confronted by a dimpled cleric with wavy hair holding a cross, that we are supposed to cringe in front of it? Well, you may have crinkled in its presence, but I have never done so. The report that is in my central dossier—that before the cross I experienced nausea, dizziness, and a certain creeping sensation, like the memory of ants marching over a limb long severed—is a libel!

Yes, she got the job. The creative director called her back for another interview. Again she impressed him and offered to do some commercials on speculation. He gave her packets of information about aluminum products that wouldn't pit and

. . . .

plastic products that shouldn't melt and asked her to write two sixty-second commercials for each.

Gladly she accepted the assignment, and skippingly she went right to the Lutheran church to express her thanks. I could have distracted her easily if I hadn't already taken both Blister and Glister off the case, but I continued to monitor her activity televisionally.

It has always amazed me how the Supernal Enemy gets extravagant thanks for favors granted when they were mere coincidences. She no more got that job as a result of her prayer to the Enemy than I got America as a graduation present from *Schola Temptorum*. More amazing still is that the Enemy rewards this clumsy girl's thanks for the favor granted with yet another favor. He will give it to her even though she hasn't asked for it and may not like it when He does give it. That kind of unrequested generosity would turn my stomach if I had one.

If I were to guess what benison he will bestow on her, I would think it a bibliography of those wayward creatures in the past who have wandered in from the cold to our Enemy's all-suffocating warmth. Or perhaps it will be a highlighting of her already vast reading in literature, enabling her to recall all sorts of Christian sparklers, a diamelle here, a marca-

. . . .

site there, glints from the past from which to build the glitz of the present.

Rumbustiously yours,

Fleetwood

XI

Most scabrous Uncle,

Saturday morning I slept late and woke up with a headache. I had spent a particularly tedious week at a theological convention, watching academicians take sides, taunt each other, and eventually come to blows. Liberals were bullish, beating conservatives over the head for investing too much in faith and too little in intellect. Bearish, conservatives fought back, contending that the intellect was bankrupt and that only faith will pay dividends in the life to come.

It was quite comic really, the whole affair coming to a head on morning television: the liberal theologian in shirt and tie, looking like an East German

. . . .

spy caught with his hand in the cookie jar; the conservative theologian in collar and rabat, clutching the jar for dear life, not willing to share his cookies with the liberal theologian until he learned to behave himself.

Little does each side know that it is not the far left or the far right who controls the world but the extreme middle, and that in the middle the sword sheathed in stone is metaphor. He who wrests it from the lapidary scabbard and wields it over his head can command the peoples of the earth.

By noon, the theological lint brushed from my clothes, I dressed and stepped out into the November sun. Walking along Central Park South at a fairly brisk pace, I soon recovered my good spirits. At the St. Moritz Hotel whom did I see but Fido standing in front, his expression not a happy one. I knew he had a luncheon date with my darling young temptand, and though I had arrived on time and he had arrived on time, she hadn't. He walked back and forth outside, his impatience rising. I turned into the lobby and walked to Rumpelmayer's, a restaurant whose name was redolent of rapscallion creatures from the dark side of the imagination. Knowing that she would not appear for some minutes yet, I allowed myself to be seated and ordered a cranberry juice on the rocks.

Twenty minutes must have passed before they

. . . .

entered the dining room. He was furious; she was not particularly hungry; soon his appetite got the better of him, and he was drooling over the menu, which featured such hideous delights as Peach Melba and Cassis Hélène. Ice cream was a force for good in the world, he maintained, ordering a banana split. She asked for a large cookie with nuts and a cup of coffee, eager to talk about a discovery she had made during the week at the New York Public Library.

Had he ever been in the Berg Collection? she asked.

No, he answered, but he knew that it was on the third floor.

Had he ever read *The Screwtape Letters?*

Yes, he had, he answered with his mouth full of that awful gelid material. Assigned reading in high school. It was the correspondence of a senior devil instructing a junior devil on how to tempt a soul. Rather dull, he recalled.

Well, she had just discovered it, the original manuscript in the Berg Collection, handwritten from margin to margin, in a brown envelope . . .

It was available in paperback, he couldn't resist saying.

How was she to know? A friend of hers had recommended it and told her where to get it. But that

. . . .

was all beside the point. When she did read it, she found that it made the most preposterous claim.

What was that? he asked as the interior of his mouth began to feel like frozen yarn.

The author claimed not only that God existed but also that the Devil existed. What do you make of that? she asked.

I'm not surprised, he said, wiping the whipped cream from his slithering lips.

Now I can't say that I am pleased that the avuncular correspondence to my friend Wormwood has appeared in book form, especially when it gives such an unflattering portrait of an uncle, yet it gives me some pleasure to know that it demonstrates, apparently quite convincingly to those with a metaphoric turn of mind, that the Infernal World does indeed exist and that toiling in it are practitioners of some substance like Wormwood and me.

How did she know that it just wasn't a literary convention? asked her green-corduroyed friend. After all, the Devil has appeared in literature from time to time. He cited two longish epic poems, one in the seventeenth century by a blinded Englishman who had to dictate the pentameters to his daughters, the other in the fourteenth century by an Italian who wound his way down into Hell as though he were roller-skating down the Guggenheim.

. . . .

No, said my temptand animatedly, she no longer thought the Devil a literary concoction and felt sure she had seen his fine infernal hand on more than one occasion in her life. But why was the Devil, the faction or the fiction, so unpopular with sophisticated moderns?

That was easy, said her friend. The Devil no longer goes about roaring like a lion, seeking whom he may devour. Rather he dresses in pinstripe suit, buttoned-down shirt, silk rep tie, and carries a leather attaché case with combination lock, making his calls, always phoning ahead, in a quiet, businesslike way.

Did he know this for sure? she asked.

No, he said; of all the Christian teachings the idea of a personal devil stretched credibility the most. (For this remark he shall pay dearly!)

Saying it was her turn, she picked up the bill at the restaurant. Since she was making more money than he, she said it was only fair. "Diabolic" was the word he used to describe her action, but he went along with it quite easily, even criticizing her for not leaving a large enough tip.

Little did they realize, as they walked along Central Park South, that devils change their metaphors prismatically with the rotation of the earth and the revolution of society. Even as the couple walked hand in hand down Fifth Avenue—I really do dislike

. . . .

this romantic mush—I was strolling behind them, windowshopping, eavesdropping on their conversation, and strategizing my next move.

If only I could keep them out of bookstores, I would make my task easier. Like filings to magnets, however, they turned into Doubleday's, and into Scribner's, into Brentano's and into Rizzoli's. I would have cause to worry if I had not read all the books in these stores already and knew which passages in them were suitable for temptation.

It's a shame, dear Uncle, that you have read so little; you had so much time on your hands at the college.

Disrespectfully yours,

Fleetwood

XII

Most sulfuric Uncle,

Your inability to swallow the fact that I have read everything in a bookstore—or in a library, for that matter—was typical of your narrow-mindedness. My marks at *Schola Temptorum* were never the best, and I may never have risen from the lower half of the class to the upper, but still I was the pupil that books made an impression upon. If you were to reassemble our class today, you would find that I am the only one who still reads books out of intellectual curiosity.

And how, you would certainly ask, if you had not lost your ability to speak, am I able to read a store or a library full of books? I took a speed-reading course, if you must know, and am now able to

. . . .

peruse, with the speed of laser lighting, encyclopedias of philosophy and theology and indeed of everything else. What will annoy you the more, I'm sure, is that I am able to retain almost photographically everything that I have read.

One side benefit of this course is that I have invited a few friends to read with me the great books of theism and atheism, of angelism and diabolism. Next Sunday—what better day of the week to meet?—we are gathering at my place to blitzkrieg through Nietzsche. It will be slow-going, even at high velocity, and I'm not sure how much of him I want to retain, but the reading keeps my rented retinas nimble.

That you may not think me entirely negative, I must express my gratitude for at least one thing long ago at the college. Although I fear to say it because it may make your coals glow a little longer, your *Index Librorum Prohibitorum* was an inspired idea. That padlocked section of the library where you stashed the forbidden books—I remember we called it Heaven—saved us from having to plow through such tedious tomes as *The Imitation of Christ* and *The Practice of the Presence of God.*

Of course, in rebelling against your authority, I have eventually read these and all the other books that were under lock and key. Indeed, I have always kept two or three such volumes on my night table so

. . . .

that whenever I am unable to sleep, whether from the heartbreak of psoriasis or the heartburn of psychiatry, I have them right to hand. They provide marvelous distraction, putting me to sleep in five minutes' time.

Yes, the temptand did eventually buy her own copy of *The Screwtape Letters.* I hurried ahead of her into every bookstore she approached, rearranging the stock on the shelves and covering the *Letters* with other titles. That was on the weekend. During the week, when she was on her own, she found an exposed copy in Greenwich Village. Since then, she has read it more than once, each time musing about the existence of such practitioners of the infernal art as Screwtape and Wormwood and such code names as Uncle and Nephew.

This past weekend was particularly enjoyable for me. I got to put on some costumes and frolic about in the snow. Christmas, that vile feast, is fast approaching, as you know, but as you cannot possibly know, the sidewalks of Manhattan are dotted with hireling Santas ringing bells and inviting passersby to drop some coins into kettles hanging from tripods.

Well, this Saturday past I invited a Santa into a dark alley and asked for his suit. When he refused, I appropriated it anyway, leaving him as refuse on a trash bin, and sauntered back to his stand on Park

. . . .

Avenue. I did not have long to wait for them, she trying against her very nature to improve in punctuality, Fido managing to dampen his impatience by stopping at every hydrant.

Approaching, she was furrily wrapped against the cold; he was jauntily attired, his trench coat unbuttoned, his head bare. I shivered and rang my bell as I stepped in front of them, asking them—I could hardly say the words—to remember God's poor in some monetary way this holy season. She reached out and snapped my beard. Where's the holiday spirit? I shouted. He pulled off his mother's mittens, for that was where he kept his coins, and threw them into the kettle. Embarrassed, she pulled him away, demanding to know if he were going to stop at every man in a red suit who stuck his hand out. Probably, he said.

As they walked by St. Bartholomew's, I approached them again, this time in the guise of a beggar, who had been so benumbed by the cold that he didn't notice my swiping his loathsome clothes. Leaving the wretch in his corrugated cardboard lair, I approached the couple in my rags and—swallowing hard at what I was about to say—asked in Jesus' sweet name for some money to get something to eat. She turned away, revulsed at the very sight of me, but he reached into his pocket and gave me a bill, the only bill in his wallet.

. . . .

Ahead of her friend in the falling snow, she challenged him to a race, beating him to the Brasserie by half a city block. Not only did they want to get something to eat, they also needed to get warm, for the wind was picking up. When she asked over onion soup, her spoon breaking through the crust of French bread and broiled cheese, releasing the aroma of old Provence, what the devil (I liked her expression) he thought he was doing out there, he explained that it was the old cup-of-cold-water theory. If you gave something, even a cup of cold water, in the Supernal One's name, then you were giving it to the Supernal One Himself.

"Do you really expect me to believe that?" she asked.

"It's both as simple and as complex as that," he said as he finished the salad. "You'll find it in the New Testament. By the way, do you have a copy in Latin? I'd lend you my Greek one, only you don't read Greek—the one chink in your educational armor."

When the waiter brought the check, the corduroyed one found his wallet empty and asked if she would be so kind as to pay it.

"Well, of all the stupid things!" she shouted and stormed into the snowy night, leaving her friend

. . . .

to work something out with the maître d'hôtel, who was full of nasty questions.

Now at last I have separated her from the one person who in the past few weeks has influenced her in the wrong direction. In the weekends to come I shall close in for the kill.

I know you despise gifts, dear Uncle, although I can never imagine your having been deluged with them at any time in your life, but I am giving you one anyway. Before you cry out against the crass commercialization of this giving time of year, let me say that I did not buy it or acquire it by any shady means. I wrote it myself, a little booklet, and had it printed at my own expense. Perhaps someone at the home will read it to you by the fire.

Disparagingly yours,

Fleetwood

Most jaundiced Uncle,

How dare you criticize me for invoking the name of the Supernal One! I, too, find it almost unutterable, but I did it for a reason, and as it turned out, it was quite effective. In fact, not only was I standing in for a sidewalk Santa but also I was impersonating the Second Person of the Supernal Trinity and getting away with it, deserving an Academy Award for my performance, I should think. The temptand and her faithful Irish setter haven't spoken for a week and do not plan to get together this weekend.

I suppose you haven't had time yet to look at the booklet I sent you. Even if you had, I don't think you'd tell me. Jealousy is a terrible thing in a mentor,

. . . .

turning one the color of crème de menthe and giving off about the same pharmaceutical odor.

My temptand planned a quiet weekend around her apartment, intending to read some books (I had the foresight to mark some salient passages) and attempt some recipes (her regional appetites are revolting to one brought up on the pleasures of British cuisine).

Able to relax, therefore, for the first time in a long while, I paid some attention to my personal correspondence, which I handle by fountain pen. What is difficult to find these days in paper with enough cotton in it to prevent my inks from laddering or with too hard a finish for the inks to be absorbed at all. I am experimenting now with a variety of nibs, trying to add to my skills the art of italic and other cursive alphabets. What I am tyring to achieve is a certain look, a letter of substance that is attractively transcribed, a collectible really . . . which is not at all how your correspondence to me looked, all cramped and crimped, scrawled and scratched.

Yes, I shall admit it before you charge me. I am vain about my handwriting and shall continue to be so, even though I have just invested in a word processor with letter-quality printer—these letters to you have been produced on this computer—that can type about as fast as I can think. Playing about with

. . . .

the keyboard and terminal, I realized that I haven't had so much fun since I learned to play the organ. By the way, I am not one of those who find the pen and the processor mutually incompatible, although the former has a tendency to leak at high altitudes and the latter is subject to short circuit.

My temptand just got a telephone call—yes, I have tapped her line, the technology being readily available in government manuals—it was from that dogged friend of hers. Fido had sent her some crazy cards in the mail, attempting to heal the ruptured friendship; they arrived on Saturday afternoon and now, well after dinnertime, he has telephoned, asking her to meet him at St. Patrick's Cathedral.

She accepted—rather too quickly, I thought—and leaving behind some half-read Bertrand Russell and some half-eaten Bananas Foster, threw her coat on. She bounded down the stairs of her brownstone—she lives on the third floor—but I managed to catch her heel on a piece of worn carpet: she fell with a scream to the landing below. I thought that would bring her to her senses and make her crawl back up to her room. But no, the frazzled girl, howling with pain, used the railing to get out the door and down the front steps. Limping, she set out across town toward the church.

Desperate to prevent her arrival, I spread

. . . .

patches of ice on the sidewalk; I sent taxicabs hurtling at her as she crossed Park Avenue; I blew from west to east across the island of Manhattan, my cheeks puffed like the Winds at corners of old cartography; but onward toward the cathedral she limped. She made it, just barely, to a bronze door and attempted to pull it open. I pulled against her on the other side, but someone leaving the church—whatever happened to Christian charity?—pushed me aside, and she managed to slip in.

The cathedral is a great Gothic barn of a place, I don't mind telling you, and filled with feathery presences, my angelic counterparts, crowding about and calling me stinky names, asking what business I had in this holy place. Monkey business, I said, and told them to shuffle off, mind their own business while I took care of mine. They were rude at first, but then they became rough; they flung me to the floor and stomped on me, and just when they were going to force me to embrace the cruciform, I shouted that I had a license to tempt and if only they would let me reach into my pocket. . . . They backed off a little, reluctantly, looking at each other in disbelief, leaving me just enough room to maneuver.

It was cold, but not so cold as it was on the outside. The votive candles gave off little heat, most of them having been electrified. Steam careened

. . . .

through the pipes. Ladies of the evening warmed their bodies against the wall radiators or over the floor vents before hitting the pavement again in search of pleasure and profit.

She couldn't find her friend anywhere in the columned precincts. The place was so large that there was a good chance they would miss each other in the semidarkness. Then it was that my nose detected the lingering fumes of incense recently burned. I tried to prevent it, pinching my nose until the blood ran, but then I sneezed. She turned around but didn't see me. Instead she saw Fido at the other end of the church. He ran to her. When they embraced, I thought I would be sick.

With her leaning on him, they walked around the place. First, he took her to the back of the main altar and showed her the stairs downward, not to the cache of weapons being stored for the revolution against the Protestants but to the vault where the previous archbishops of New York lay buried. She smiled in her pain and said that the firepower was probably stored under the side altars.

Then he brought her down the side aisles, looking behind the altars for evidence of grenades and bazookas and automatic weaponry, ending up in front of Rose of Lima and Stanislaus Kostka. Looking up at the sixteenth-century saints who had died in

. . . .

their teens, he had the nerve to confabulate the story that Rosie and Stanny, seeing as how they were on adjoining pedestals, had become friends over the years, and that during Holy Week, when their statues were shrouded in purple, they actually flew to the Virgin Islands for some rest and recreation, returning in time for the sumptuous liturgies on Holy Saturday and Easter Sunday. I couldn't believe what I was hearing! Legend, she asked? Legend, he said, with a truth all its own. And she began to laugh.

The Hebrew Scriptures have recorded an army's being slain with the jawbone of an ass, but how this simpleton was able to woo my Phi Beta Kappa away from me with a fib was a mystery. It is only a temporary victory, though, and you should not taunt me for it, for I shall be victorious in the end. I shall spend next week composing an alternate legend and shall present it to her under whatever guise next weekend.

Do stop sniveling. Carcinoma tells me that your complaints run as fast as your nose. Enclosed, please find six boxes of facial tissue. I know you detest the products of commercial imagination, but each box, and the tissue contained in it, is tinted in a different color, one sheet popping up after another, each sheet being softer and thicker than the ones available in Dimchurch. They may not stop the drippage and

. . . .

seepage, but—cheer up!—they will make your nose less red from the blowing.

Exasperatingly yours,

Fleetwood

XIV

Most rabid Uncle,

I have spent the week recovering from the beating I took at the cathedral last Saturday night. The fact that we are incorporeal spirits does not lessen the pain when one's rented corpus is thumped and bumped about by a bevy of angelic bouncers. Beefsteak on the black and blue patches is the only remedy that seems to work, and if it had not been "Obsession Week" on late-night television, I do not think I could have survived. Anyway, I should have known better than to have gone into that place by myself. I am already planning a return engagement, bringing with me some mercenaries, the Superfly and

. . . .

the Junk Yard Dog, the Road Warriors and the Midnight Express: we shall tear the place apart!

In the meantime, I plan to continue my recuperation right through to the next weekend. Fido has gone northward to Boston, where his parents are kenneled; they will cuff him about for a couple of days as only a mother and father can.

In the meantime, during the day, I am working on my book, the first draft of which I sent you in pamphlet form some weeks back. It is entitled *The Joyful Atheist.* It is meant to be an alternative work to *The Joyful Christian,* the book filled with selections from the writings of C. S. Lewis of unhappy memory. My book will contain snippets from the writings of those people in the history of the world who, hopefully, have found satisfaction in a life of unbelief.

Very few writers, I must say, have written believably about what they don't believe. It may be that language *qua* language does not admit of unbelief. But the principle of contradiction is as much our tool as theirs, and I intend to use it tellingly. The fact that we ourselves are confirmed theists, of course, is something that few Christians dwell upon, but our brand of theism is, mark you, particularly difficult to market. Hence my attempt to produce an attractive and convincing volume. If you have any suggestions, I would appreciate your communicating them to Carcinoma,

. . . .

who tells me that, although you cannot speak, you are able to wheeze a lot, making dot-and-dash-like sounds.

My temptand is spending much time with a Church-of-England-in-America person who hopes to bag her for his communion. He is long on learning but short in piety, so I have little to fear from him. No doubt, he will introduce her to a clergyperson who will volunteer to explain to her the history and the liturgy and the seeming ambiguity of their doctrinal belief. His efforts I shall be able to sabotage easily.

One point about books. I think in a previous letter I exaggerated the power of certain titles in ascetical theology to put me to sleep. Actually, quite the opposite is the case. They keep me awake and stimulate me to an extraordinary degree, not because I agree with their theses but because many of them are so agreeably written. Why is it that those who try to make atheism or agnosticism appealing write so flumsily?

One thing the philosophers and theologians have failed to note is that diabolists like you and me find much of the interpretation of human history irrelevant. For example, when at a recent theological convention I read a paper contending that the Reformation never happened . . . or if indeed it did happen, it had no significance, I was laughed from the

. . . .

hall. The reason is simple, of course, that we diabolists neither gain nor lose ground when a believer switches from one brand of belief to another. It is much the same, I am given to understand, with smoking cigarettes.

What we must do is inculcate unbelief, which is hard for us to do, confirmed theists that we are. But what is the product? Hopefully, we are hawking a thousand of them, in bright packages with alluring names and promising contents, but in reality what we are huckstering is despair. Which is why I began using state-of-the-art marketing and packaging techniques. Despair is not easy to market, but try we must. . . .

It is Sunday night as I sit down to Tandy, the name I have given my word processor. My temptand has returned to her apartment, carrying a book given to her earlier in the day by her Episcopalian friend. *Mere Christianity* is its title. It is no stranger to me; nor should it be to you. Next to the Bible, it is the single most deleterious volume read in America. Hopefully, my temptand will set the book down on a table and forget its whereabouts. Better, she may put it into one of her bottomless handbags—she has tens of them—where it will be lost forever.

Because you never attempted the fair sex during your temptorial career, you have never had the

. . . .

pleasure of delving into that treasure trove known as a woman's handbag. In it one finds powder for the face, gloss for the lips, thickener for the lashes, liner for the lids, and a small mirror for viewing the whole mess. There is a wallet full of money and a case full of credit cards to huge department stores and smart specialty shoppes. A Week-at-a-Glance book there surely is, with birthdays noted and appointments scribbled, a packet of photographs of parents and boyfriends, a subway map, and a railroad schedule. Sometimes there are stimulants or depressants, and when none of them work, antacids that fizz and froth. At the very bottom one uncovers a paperback book, with cover creased and pages rumpled, retailing a historical romance or a romantic fantasy. All in all, when spread across a table, the articles make a remarkable anthropological statement, being as they are a survival kit for the contemporary working woman stranded on a leafless, lawnless island.

Be resigned to your fate. Ash in the grate you shall be. It is what awaits us all.

Derisively yours,

Fleetwood

XV

Most devious Uncle,

So you think I use the word "hopefully" too much. Realistically, what you meant to say is that you didn't think it a proper English usage, that one should not have begun a sentence with what appeared to be a dangling adverb. Unfortunately for you, it is not dangling at all; it is an absolute, in the manner of genitive absolutes in Greek and ablative absolutes in Latin. Grammatically, it may be construed as an adverbial absolute, not syntactically connected to the sentence, but rather indicating the timber or tone of the voice or pen of the writer or speaker. Hopefully, you will never question me on this usage again.

What can you do to stop the export of *Mere*

. . . .

Christianity to America? Nothing probably, since you are a burned-out case yourself, but somebody in England must be able to do something to staunch the flow of that doctrinal tripe to America! As many as one hundred thousand copies of this seditious volume are flooding American bookstores each year. Christians have it in their libraries. Converts have it in their pockets and purses. Even decorators position, tastefully, the anniversary edition on the coffee tables of their Christian clients. Gideons are probably at this very moment slipping copies of it into every motel room in North America.

You put it on the *Index Librorum Prohibitorum* at the college. But if you really wanted to condemn it to obscurity, you should have had it reviewed lukewarmly, suggesting that it would make agnostics curious, that it should be in every atheist's library, that the truly godless can sleep peacefully if lumpily with a copy of it under their pillow.

I know you will plead that you were the one gloriously responsible for matching the physical characteristics of the paperback edition with the obsolescence of the Christianity itself. But did you really think that type the size of footnotes, glue the consistency of broth, and paper smelling of pulp would destroy the circulation of the work? If anything, these

. . . .

physical characteristics have turned it into a cultic phenomenon.

Why Americans find the book so attractive I have no idea. Only a few think it is a compendium, a basic minimum, a catechism without questions and answers, of what people must believe if they want to live as Christians. Most think it is a summary of what they may conveniently believe, or not believe, and still be called Christians.

But what fuddles me is that Americans hate catechetical works. *Mere Christianity* is plain fare honestly prepared, but it must be eaten slowly, chewed, digested, thought through. But Americans want their apologetics like their food: fast, dressed or sauced with vegetables or gravy, with lots of preservatives and perhaps one or another minimum daily requirement missing.

Mere Christianity, on the other hand, seems to have become an essential ingredient in the American spiritual diet. Every time I think of it, I want to reach for one of my temptand's antacids to relieve my soulburn. But relief comes only when I help the mass-marketing of the work, the quicker to saturate the readership and to send a warehouse full of unsold copies to the remainder houses, or better, to the Philippines.

If there is a lesson to be learned here, pri-

. . . .

vately that is to say among us diabolists, it is that *Mere Christianity* has enough spiritual energy to light up the souls of American Christians for the next two hundred years. Once I was able to admit this, I developed a counterstrategy. What I needed was a book like it, not a refutation of it, but a creative and forceful presentation of what we infernals believed and how we behaved. (I have had to abandon *The Joyful Atheist;* I just couldn't find enough material.)

I had at first thought of encouraging an articulate academic or a lazy cleric to write the work. There are not a few of them around, but each has such an unattractive personal life as to disqualify him as spokesperson for the cause.

"Give me a bite of your grapefruit—I gave you a bite of mine!" That's the way I would begin the work, I inevitably having to be the ghostwriter. From the fact that you didn't give me a bite of yours, I can induce the unfairness of human behavior in general and dangle from it a daisy chain of syllogisms proving wronghood as the essential clue to the meaning of the universe. If one doesn't mind a squirt in the eye every now and then, the argument from citrus can be quite effective.

With this sort of exposition, I have put together a rather snappy proposal, which I have sent in a glazed orange box to publishers whom I feel would

. . . .

be receptive to *Mere Diabolism,* as the work is tentatively entitled. It could also be called *Diabolism for Everybody.*

To date I have not gotten an acceptance. All I've received are polite if negative notes like "Thank you, but no thank you"; "This is only one publisher's opinion"; and "Do you really expect to earn money by writing such short paragraphs?"

Perhaps I'll publish it myself.

Whichever, you will get one of the first copies, whether you want it or not.

Vengefully yours,

Fleetwood

XVI

Most bilious Uncle,

Of course I know that *Mere Christianity* is not being exported from England. Did you think I didn't know that? What are you trying to prove? That I don't know that it is published in New York? I know all there is to know about *Mere Christianity,* and it is making me metaphorically sick to my stomach. Not only is it a mindless book that mindless people are buying to buttress their mindless faith, it is also an intellectually harmful book, suggesting as it does that one should forsake one's intellect in order to believe. My poor temptand was in a tizzy after reading it, not knowing what to think, what to believe.

. . . .

Everything would have proceeded on schedule, like an electric train on a circular track, if Fido hadn't come sniffing along to insist that to be a Christian one had to believe only in a few things, maybe only four or five. That seemed to calm the temptand down. Press her though I did, I could not get her to ask her flea-ridden friend just what those four or five things were. I shall be working on this in the weeks to come. Once articulated, these terms will be easily destroyed.

This weekend past—I am writing again on Sunday night—the temptand spent some time with an Episcopalian priest, who instructed her with the sureness of grasp of one who had presided at the Council of Nicaea. She left his apartment as if intoxicated with creeds.

Sunday afternoon she spent with Fido because she wanted to discuss the articles in the creed and—alas—because she was falling in love with him; there was even some talk of children. Have you ever noticed that people can discuss a creed for only so long before they have to change the subject? After serving grits and grillades, she turned on the FM-stereo station, hoping to find some romantic music; instead, it was broadcasting something particularly mournful. Smetana's *Moldau,* he said; it reminded him of death

. . . .

because he had first heard it in the company of a friend who had since died.

They talked of death; he seemed calm about it, accepting as truth everything the Christian religion had to say about it. She, however, was uneasy. Death seemed so interruptive and the destination after death seemed so imprecise. He, on the other hand, had the audacity to say that if one truly believed that death was not an end but a beginning, then death would be desirable, and the sooner it happened, the better. And that if she insisted on serving coffee laced with chicory, his death would be very soon indeed.

There had been a lot of talk about death at her advertising agency. It seemed that two young account executives were killed in midweek by a falling chimney which happened to be on the roof of a brownstone in the middle of Manhattan; they were relaxing after work, as it were, with a couple of scantily clad young women before going home to their wives and children in New Jersey. Was that some kind of divine punishment? she demanded to know. He refused to call it that, saying that divine mercy knew no bounds. He did point out, though, that their unseemly deaths lacked spiritual style.

She never wanted to die, she said, and on that point I shall work in the weeks to come. Temerity, fearfulness, is the pinhole that with the right pressure

. . . .

can become a wind tunnel shaking her very being and bringing her to spiritual ruin. What I would like to do is put him, as the popular song has it, alone "on a slow boat to China."

I do wish you weren't so infirm. I would like to fly you to New York so that you might see at firsthand how a large-scale temptorial operation in the New World works. Perhaps in the spring, when the weather is better. Everything here is ice and wind, snow and sleet. At least there's central heating, which is more than I can say of England.

Yours toastily,

Fleetwood

XVII

Most scurrilous Uncle,

At the risk of giving you pleasure when you deserve only pain, I will tell you that this past weekend, instead of paying attention to my temptand, I was summoned by Opposite Number to lunch. I know better now than to try to avoid such a rendezvous . . .

Hence when I got the telephone call early on Saturday morning, I accepted as smoothly as my sleepy voice would allow. But when he suggested Trattoria Archangelico's at noon, I made a counter-suggestion, even though I knew that Salmonella, an undercover operative of mine, was maître d' there. Much to my surprise, he agreed to meet me at one

. . . .

o'clock at a place that is more my turf than his, the Russian Tea Room.

This was history in the making, for he had never before accepted a countersuggestion from me. Perhaps he wanted to exchange holiday gifts, I thought as I walked west on Fifty-third Street. In order not to be embarrassed, I darted into Harper & Row's bookstore and made a purchase. Waiting to have it giftwrapped caused me to arrive at the Tea Room at one-thirty.

At the best of times, Opposite Number is testy, but today he was positively detestable as I joined him at a table by the window. After some very unfunny remarks about his slumming on West Fifty-seventh Street and about how one gets to Carnegie Hall ("Pray, mister; pray!"), we had the most unusual conversation.

"I'm worried."

"About what?"

"About us."

"Then we should stop meeting this way."

"That's not what I mean." He had chopped liver to start, and I had jellied calves' feet. "Do you believe in fairies?"

"It's always seemed to me that when humankind didn't know how to explain something, it had a tendency to generate humanoidal creatures as part of

. . . .

the counterexplanation. Sometimes the creatures were little people . . ."

"It's bigger than that," said Opposite Number, sending his fork into Shashlik Caucasian; for all his anxiety, his appetite seemed unabated.

"What do you want?" I asked, filling my mouth with Côtelette à la Kiev, "a complete rehearsal of the mythologies of the West?"

"No, it's more complicated than that," he said. "Do you, as you go about your daily round, experience a diminution of belief in angels *qua* angels?"

"Well, I certainly feel that I can parade around pretty much as I please—at least around the big cities—without fear of being recognized on the streets, if that's what you mean."

"What I'm getting at, and you're certainly not making it any easier, is that belief in angels, both good angels and—ahem—bad angels, is being phased out at the seminaries in the liturgical-intellectual tradition, that we're being dismissed as Persian accretions, that greeting-card artists have made us figures of fun, rouging our cheeks, baring our bottoms, depicting us with Cupid-like rascality in amatory affairs. All theology is by its very nature defective, full of fakes and fissures," I can remember his saying with precision, "but we are *not* to be found among those stinking pieces of *trompe-l'oeil* in the liberal theolo-

. . . .

gian's warehouse." He didn't know what would become of us all, he said, tears falling into his farinaceous dessert.

I could never in my wildest dreams have imagined such a situation, I having to cheer up my Opposite Number! Our Supernal Lord, who no doubt was watching us on closed-circuit television, must have been gagging during the whole horrid scene!

It is perhaps ironic that I am better read than my Opposite Number, but I did point out that there was at least one contemporary intellectual who felt that the existence of angelic creatures was not only emotionally desirable but also intellectually possible. *The Angels and Us* he had not read, nor had he heard of the author, an American philosopher of Jewish parentage and Aristotelian intellect. When I said that I would lend him my copy, it was as though I had dropped sugar cubes into his teacup. He relaxed and said that he was most grateful, even to the point of picking up the quite substantial check. He leaned back in his chair with what seemed like blessed relief. "Pinions have always looked well on me," he said with some satisfaction.

I could have warned him, I suppose, about what threatened him from behind, but I didn't. He leaned too far back and fell over, his head hitting a samovar and upending it, scalding Russian tea

. . . .

splashing all over him. I tiptoed toward the door as discreetly as I could.

What is the world coming to? I thought as I walked past Carnegie Hall, pausing for a moment in the doorway to open my elegantly wrapped present. A book it was, *Introduction à la vie dévote,* bound in white leather with ribbon marker and gilt edges. His gaucherie was exceeded only by my own. I had given him *Les fleurs du mal* with lots of salacious watercolors.

Carcinoma tells me that Dimchurch this winter has never been more damp, more bitter, what with much of the weather coming off the North Sea. Hence I am sending with this missive a sweater. Olive drab I remember as your favorite color, the color of the camouflage sweaters used by the S.A.S. commando regiment in your war. Hence I sending you a scarlet one woven of ranch mink and merino wool, knowing that it will not only keep you warm but also embarrass you.

Yours animiverously,

Fleetwood

Most rapacious Uncle,

How amusing, your account of first dining with the Opposite Number assigned to you! I did not realize that the existence of ON's was classified information. How disarming was that first revelation of his existence! How devastating is revelation of any kind!

How doubly startling my lunch was; it virtually destroyed last weekend for me! The advances I had made against my darling young temptand have nearly been destroyed in my absence. I don't know how she did it, but in a mere two weeks' time she has discovered prayer. No, not biblical prayer or liturgical prayer—I can handle those with ease—but contemplative prayer.

. . . .

When I looked in on her last night—Saturday night; I couldn't arrive much before nine—I found the door to her apartment open. Everything within was in disarray—dishes piled high, newspapers scattered about, garbage unemptied—as though there had been a robbery in the place, perhaps even a rape. But it was worse than that. There she was, kneeling in the middle of the floor, her arms outstretched in that accursed cruciform.

She seemed quite absorbed, quite rapt in what she was doing, trying no doubt to communicate with the Supernal One. I could have tempted her with distractions, I suppose. I could have generated enough static to jam her heavenly broadcast. That is what you would have done, I know, and that indeed is what is recommended in the *Regulae Temptorum.* That rancid course of action, however, and you know it, has never worked!

More effective, but certainly not the last word in this sort of situation, is to let the body take its own course. Her arms would tire in time, her thighs throb, her sinews knot, and her body would, after not too many minutes, begin to droop, rather like an airplane going into a spinning dive: exhilarating at first, giddying even, but as the earth comes rushing up, you pretty quickly come to your senses and pull out of it with a terrible whine.

. . . .

Seeing her thus occupied, I thought I'd take advantage of the few minutes I had to look around for clues as to what she had been doing this past couple of weeks and perhaps what I should be doing next week.

Close to her on the floor, spines broken, facing pages lying flat, were paperback copies—I do think one should read the classics in hardcover and in the original languages!—of *Dark Night of the Soul* and *The Interior Castle.* Both had page corners creased and passages marked. No doubt what she was trying to do was re-create in one night the history of contemplative prayer *à la espagnole.*

The telephone rang. She didn't seem to hear it. I didn't think I would do great harm by picking up the receiver and listening. Fido was yelping at the other end. From what I was able to gather, he was there earlier in the evening, had dinner with her, and after an argument was told to leave; he, poor blubbering fool, was trying to make up.

In the plastic bag by the sink was a garbologist's delight, the remains of their dinner: bits and pieces of chicken, lobster, shrimp, clams, mussels. The smell of saffron and the sticky rice scorched in a frying pan led me to conclude that she had served *paella* and that in an orgy of Spanish mysticism had

. . . .

flung her friend out into the night and plunged herself into an all-night prayer vigil.

The telephone rang again. Again I lifted the receiver to my ear. It was Fido, this time protesting that she should not—as she had apparently threatened to do earlier in the evening—go out into the ice and snow to kneel—she could have been a great actress if she weren't so shy—in the doorway of some church for all the city to see. As I put the instrument back onto its cradle, I heard him sputtering something to the effect that spirituality should be stylish but not ostentatious.

Still she remained motionless, her eyes closed, her lips moving as if with words. No, before you even ask, I did not eavesdrop on her transmission. I didn't have to. I could hear it clear across the room. "Father Mother God," she said over and over again. My, she didn't get that from the Spanish mystics!

Any minute now she would drop, and so for amusement—it was now around midnight—I put a platter from a Temptations album on the stereo and started to look through her handbag again, pulling out one thing after another and putting it on her writing table. The credit cards I hid in books on her shelf, some in Mrs. Dull, others in Mrs. Eddy. In her Week-at-a-Glance book, I jotted down my own birthday. At the very bottom of the bag, I found tattered

. . . .

paperback copies of—my, she is really looking for trouble!—*The Hymns of Charles Wesley* and *The Power of Positive Thinking.*

Next thing I knew—I must have dropped off—it was dawn. To my amazement she was still there in the middle of the floor; it was probably the saffron and the rice interacting chemically to form a sort of starch that held her in place. Her hands were by her side, her eyes were still closed, but her mouth still moved as if with words of prayer—"Father Mother God," she seemed to be repeating—if I read her words correctly. My, my, I can remember thinking to myself, I should have to take drastic measures now . . . but not before I got some more sleep. I took some of her preparations with adult-proof caps and left without disturbing her.

Do take your medicine—that's my message to you. You gave it to others long enough, and foul-tasting stuff it always was. Tempter, tempt thyself!

Yours dissolutely,

Fleetwood

XIX

Most dour Uncle,

On Saturday morning last I caught up with my temptand and her friend, walking along the beach at Coney Island. No rabbits nibbling about that frigid day, only gulls squalling, gray waves slapping wet sand and rotted piers, mischievous winds creating cathedrals in the fog, the roller coaster rising from the ocean front like a prehistoric skeleton from the misty dawn of amusement.

"What church shall I go to tomorrow?" she asked.

"You're always welcome to come to mine," said Fido.

"I'm thankful for that. But what I mean is,

. . . .

I've tried every denomination in Manhattan at least once, and I'm confused."

"Have you found any you'd like to try twice?"

"A couple. But should I go to a church because I like the beauty of its service or because, although duller than some others, it appears to me at the time to be the right one?"

I give you this snatch of dialogue, dear Uncle, because I was about to experiment with a new weapon in my arsenal. A powdery substance, it promotes *abulia nervosa,* a psychological disease that constricts one's ability to choose. Once she has ingested the substance, I am confident that she will carom from one communion to another, bounce from one church wall to another, and knock herself silly.

"Do they or don't they, those boats over there, *nuzzle* against the pier?" he asked her without warning.

"Yes and no," she said. "In one sense they appear to *nuzzle,* but in another sense they appear to *chafe.*"

"Well, you're no help. The woman I work for says that boats don't *nuzzle;* they just *float* in the water. But I say they *nuzzle;* they may even *chafe;* whichever, it's a metaphor, and some people just don't like metaphors."

I had a difficult time disguising my presence,

. . . .

there were so few people on the beach, but I managed by dint of heavy scarves and a black umbrella to keep from being discovered. At the far end of the strand they turned back. I waited for them inside Nathan's Famous and indeed took this opportunity to insert my preparation into an enormous jar on the counter.

When they came in from the cold, they ordered hot dogs, foot-long ones, mind you. She pumped a wavy line from the mustard dispenser on hers; his he slathered not only with mustard but also with relish, onions, and other drippings. Mine I had with sauerkraut—it was delicious—but I knew within moments that I would regret it.

After lunch they boarded the D train for Manhattan, and if it weren't for Lavallière, I would not have the following scraps of conversation to report. The substance I thought I had sprinkled into the mustard I had really dropped into the sauerkraut container. I stood on the blustery subway platform for days, unable to decide whether I should board the B, D, or F train, or was it the M, N, or Q train?

"How do I know which denomination is the right one? I mean, they have such conflicting claims."

"The right one is the one the Holy Spirit leads you to."

. . . .

"For that answer you win the U Thant award for ecclesial diplomacy."

"I give the Holy Spirit His due even if He is leading you away from me."

"But you don't know which direction He's leading me in."

"No, I don't."

The noise on a New York subway train is deafening, dour Uncle, and riding in one, I am unable to think two coherent thoughts in a row. But during that horrendous ride, the drug wore off, and I was able to jot down some random thoughts.

First, it does not matter which church my temptand joins, if join she must. Whether that church is liturgical or biblical, whether it believes that my existence is a creedal reality or an imagined figment, whether it waxes or wanes in membership is of no concern to me. I have keys to them all. Indeed, one key fits all.

They switched trains at Columbus Circle—to return to my reconstruction from Lavallière's tapes—and got a local to Eighty-first Street and Central Park West, where they went into the Museum of Natural History. They wanted to revisit their favorite exhibits, they said; hers, the great blue whale; his, the dinosaurs.

"How do we know that the church hasn't be-

. . . .

come extinct like some of these sea mammals down here or the land creatures upstairs."

"Are you suggesting that God is dead—long live the new technology?"

"Could that have happened?

"The evidence that God is dead, it seems to me, is not better than the evidence that God is alive. You see, it never ceases to be a matter of faith."

"I guess what I'm asking is, can a modern person go to church and really recite all that stuff in the creed?"

"The educated and cultivated people of the twentieth century, some of them, can honestly believe in the articles of the creed. I do."

"But can any of them do it happily?"

"A few."

"The saints?"

"Yes."

"But I don't want to be a saint!"

"Why not?"

"It hurts."

"Tell me about it."

"What kind of smart-alecky remark is that?"

"Can a church make rules, is that what you are asking? I think rules are only fair."

"But rules are arbitrary."

. . . .

"Some of them. Indeed, a few are even unfair."

"Why can't I just be a Christian by reading the Bible and not joining a church."

"Because then you would miss the fun of someone stealing your pocketbook from the pew, singing off-key into your ear, pushing in front of you in the communion line, being pestered for more and more money for missions and ministries you've never even heard of . . ."

"Are you saying that church is for the sinners?"

"Something like that."

"But I thought church was for the saved."

"That too."

Such mush as they talk is enough to make me lose faith in myself. Sometimes I wonder if it is worth all the effort I expend to tempt such fools. If the Supernal Lord did not value their company so much, I would not waste the effort. I wonder if, now that you are nearing your end, you feel that a life tempting such nonentities was really well spent.

Yours disconsolately,

Fleetwood

XX

Most miserable Uncle,

Your days are definitely numbered, Carcinoma has wired me, and she is scarcely able to leave your hearthside without fear of your expiring. In the attached box—I hope you admire the gift wrapping, which one now has to pay for in the specialty stores—you will find an antique cigarette lighter with an extra supply of flints and fluid. If your flame goes out, Carcinoma can, with the aid of the lighter, which you will notice is silver, administer ember-to-ember resuscitation, re-igniting you before you grow cold. Even when you are not *in extremis,* you may be able to draw some pleasure just from looking at the elephantine Ronson on the table next to you.

. . . .

My temptand, as I wrote in my last missive, has narrowed her choice of church, and between now and Easter she plans to revisit her favorites. Her enthusiasm I laugh at because in the end she will find all the churches disappointing, all the doctrines preposterous, all the clergypersons clucks. You too would laugh, if you are still able, at the dialogue during one of their perambulations around the island. Every time she asked a question, Fido had to stop at a hydrant. If I were to put all his answers into a book, which would be a very small book indeed, I think I would have the beginnings of a very good canine theology.

"But what does one do in church?" she asked. "I mean, after the liturgy or after the service."

"Pray."

"Is churchgoing everything?"

"If you're not going to church at all, then it appears to be everything. But once you start going to church, you realize that your presence there is just the beginning."

"Well, what happens after I master the service? I mean, when I know when to stand and sit, when to recite and sing, when to get money out of my pocketbook for the collection?"

"You can always pray."

"Pray? Is that all you can say? You're beginning to sound like a broken record. But I'm going to

. . . .

get to the bottom of this. What does one say when one prays? What do *you* say?"

"That's just the point. The more one prays, the less one has to say. One just gazes and admires and adores and asks what the Divine Will in one's regard is."

"It seems to me we've had this conversation before. But what happens when you get no answer?"

"Sometimes I get antsy. I have to get up—now don't laugh at me if I tell you—and juggle."

"But you don't know how to juggle!" she laughed.

"But that's just the point. I juggle, yes, but not balls or torches or anything like that—I juggle metaphors. It's what I do for a living, and although some people think it's pretty hot stuff—and I would certainly not discourage that opinion—it is pretty silly when looked at *sub specie aeternitatis.* Let me finish—I have this vision of myself juggling metaphors for the delight of the divine presence . . ."

(Let me interrupt this situation comedy, dear Uncle, with this important message. Fido is a writer; indeed, he first met the temptand at a playwriting class at the Circle in the Square Theater, where the dramaturge was writing what has since been considered the quintessential play about the American family, with characters named George and Martha. Fido

. . . .

has also acquired, because of his writing and editing skills, an editorial position with a publishing company.)

"But what about paintings that weep, statues that step off their pedestals?" she asked of her Irish setter. "What about healings of bodily ills, slayings in the spirit?"

"What about them?"

"Will they happen to me? I don't want to get hurt."

"Possibly, but not necessarily. What is sure is that something will happen and to you personally, directly, if you hang on."

"But where is Jesus in all this?"

"He's there in the Bible on the pulpit. He's there in the Host in the tabernacle. When we are talking about Him, He is with us. When someone accosts us for something, a sidewalk Santa or a curbside beggar, it is Jesus Himself in disguise."

"But how do you know this?"

"The Gospels say it's so."

"Do you believe everything in the Gospels?"

"Yes."

"Well, then, what about the theologies that have developed since the Gospels were written? All of them have defects, or so it seems to a newcomer."

"That seems to be so, but, defects or no, most

. . . .

of them still have the power to generate remarkable spiritualities or modes of communication with the Divinity."

"Are you saying that no matter what church I pick, I can't go wrong?"

"What I am saying is that no matter what church you choose, you will be better off than you are now."

"Well, that should be consoling. Instead, it's quite alarming!"

The rest of Saturday these poor creatures spent at the City Center, attending a Shavian doubleheader. In the afternoon they saw *Don Juan in Hell,* the interlude in that dreadfully long and dreary play *Man and Superman.* In the evening they saw *Saint Joan,* a chronicle play in six scenes and an epilogue. It is ironic that the play about the Devil was less to my purpose than the play about the saint; as Joan heard voices that directed her actions, so my temptand is hearing my voice and will eventually follow my directions.

This coming week, dear Uncle, I shall vary my usual *modus operandi* with regard to the temptand. To follow her, I am assigning two of my best operatives, Fester and Jester. It's not that I need their assistance —they're my crisis management team—it's just that they need the action, having to log so many hours a

. . . .

month in hot pursuit, lest they lose their diabolical edge.

Histrionically yours,

Fleetwood

XXI

Most derelict Uncle,

I don't know what preparations were in that young woman's handbag several weeks ago, the ones I ingested, but they had a powerful effect on me. I took them all, and since that time I have been dozing off and on, wreaking havoc on my national campaigns. Fortunately, my staff, under the capable direction of Tester and Titter, were able to carry on. You see, I have programmed into my computers virtually everything that is able to allure modern American males and females into unbelief. I have records and curves and rainbows on my color monitors, and I project temptational policy on a national scale with remarkable accuracy.

. . . .

In view of my temptand's sudden attraction to prayer, which seems to have multiplied like amoebae in the past five days—I know this because Palomar, from his vantage point high above Manhattan, through polished mirrors and infrared lenses, was able to peer into her apartment—I am taking drastic action.

But what a hangover I have! I should have taken her antacids too. Before my head was entirely clear this morning, Saturday morning, Fido had picked her up, and together they went to the Metropolitan Museum of Art. When I caught up with them sometime later—I mean, how much trouble can one get into with oil smeared on canvas?—he was giving her a guided tour of the religious paintings. What he specially pointed out to her were the depictions of Jesus through the centuries, which she looked at now with new eyes. There was Jesus as rabbi, as light of the gentiles, as king of kings. There was Christ crucified, the monk who ruled the world, the bridegroom of the soul. There was the poet of the spirit, the liberator, the man who belonged to the world.

Over lunch in the sculpture garden, he went over the articles in the creed, each of which she had a multitude of questions about. Over dinner that evening, which was in a Greenwich Village café, she wondered if Jesus as Bohemian had ever been de-

. . . .

picted in art. That was a Christological question, and he said that he preferred Jesus as clown—or at least, the follower of Jesus as clown—as painted by Georges Rouault, and he brought her up to date on Christology.

The biggest thrust in twentieth-century Christology, according to her friend, was the production of a Jesus that modern man could believe in. His miracles were downgraded to wishful thinking on the part of the evangelists, and the biographical details as they appeared in the Gospels had been whittled away for lack of historical veracity, appearing to be more the constructions of a literary author than an inspired writer.

"What was left?"

"A lot of ill-fitting pieces," her friend said. "Jesus is a lot like Humpty-Dumpty, you know. He has had a great fall, and all the king's men are laboring to put Him back together again."

"But will they be able to put him back together? The theologians, I mean."

"I think so. Trouble is, however, that it will take decades, maybe even centuries. And even then, he won't look the same as he did."

"That's absurd. I can't wait that long. I have to come to a decision in my lifetime. In fact, I want to make up my mind about him right now." She threw

. . . .

her napkin down and rushed out into the night. He paid the check, fortunately for him a small one, and followed her out into the street.

"These modernists," she said, "they've taken away all the pictures and conversations and left behind an empty stage, a blank screen." It was, as it turned out, Twelfth Night. "That story about the Magi—the camels and the wise men and the wandering star and the gold, frankincense, and myrrh—is it made up?"

"Yes and no," he said.

"I just knew you'd say that. But does it contain any revelatory bits?"

"You mean, like bacon bits in a salad?"

"Why is it that every time I get serious, you think of food?"

"I'm just trying to digest the complicated things you are saying."

"I opt for the story," she decided. "I am at home with metaphor. Like you, I earn my living by making metaphors. Advertising, you know, is nothing more than a series of extended metaphors. I suppose you despise that."

"It's one of the nicest things about you."

"You have to admit that truth travels along metaphor with the speed of light, does it not?"

"What do you know about electron energy?"

. . . .

"Not a great deal," she admitted, exhausted by the theological inquiries of the day. "Let's change the subject."

As they walked up Fifth Avenue, he put his mitten around her gloved hand.

"I don't live alone," he said tentatively.

"Who is she?" she asked, freeing her hand.

" 'Who are they?' is the more appropriate question."

"A harem?"

"None of them is female."

"Oh my God, don't tell me you're one of those!"

"I can't say that I am."

"How many altogether?"

"Three. And they're not of the same species."

"Cats? Dogs?"

"When I returned home one day after work, I found this creature lolling about the apartment. It resembled a tennis ball, a rather large tennis ball actually, to which were appended arms and legs and head."

"A hamster? A gerbil?"

"No, bigger than that. It had the look and the sound of a teddy bear, but of course it wasn't. I asked him who he was—I only assumed it was a he. 'Woolly,' he replied, 'Woolly Spheroid.' " The lower

. . . .

end of the avenue was deserted at this hour of the night. "Woolly is my best friend." She looked around —but saw no one to whom she could express her disbelief. "I suppose the first thing you're going to do is ask whom is he kin to?"

"No, I'm not going to ask that!" she said firmly, picking up her pace. "I ask that only when the creature is human."

"Well, you needn't worry. His lineage is long and European and full of ecclesiastics who have endured preferment through the centuries. He is, if you'd only listen, related to Augustin Cardinal Bea, who just may assign him—a little nepotism here, or is it caesaropapism?—to the apostolate of the animals. What do you think of those apples?"

"I'm not going to ask you about your *other* friends," she said frostily. "One is enough for tonight, but do let me ask you a question. Is this, this Woolly Spheroid, real, or is he a metaphor?"

"He's both."

"When can I meet him?"

"Soon."

I write this drivel to you, dear derelict Uncle, to demonstrate how difficult it is to deal with this fellow, let alone with her. I left them to their own devices for the rest of the weekend. That icy white spots had begun to appear on my exposed parts had

. . . .

nothing to do with it. There was paperwork awaiting me at my office.

Drizzle on, Uncle, and your own fluids will blot out the flamelet that still flickers in your breast. Enclosed are some desiccants that should stem the nasal tides. Take no delight in the fact that I have not yet bagged my quarry. It is the hunt that gives pleasure.

Yours sportively,

Fleetwood

XXII

Most meretricious Uncle,

Your inflammatory remarks to Carcinoma on receiving my last missive were not at all appreciated. You vastly underestimate the power of art to influence the world for good or ill. The corollary of that statement is not to take the religious art out of the museum but to put the irreligious artworks back into the museum. These latter will influence people as the former, hopefully to better results so far as we are concerned. The difficulty is what to paint.

This weekend I planned a delightful outing for my temptand and her corduroy consort. On Saturday night he took her, the Ash Wednesday smudge still visible on his forehead, to the fights, to Madison

. . . .

Square Garden, where professional wrestling—the hottest ticket in town—was on exhibition. Ahhh, the splashy entrances, the vainglorious struttings, steroidal physiques and keloidal foreheads, hair platinumed and locks lemoned, tights with tiger stripes, boots with lightning bolts—it was fan appreciation night, and the noise in the auditorium was almost deafening!

"What do you see?" Fido shouted to her.

"Two persons hitting each other and causing pain," she shouted back.

Golden men hulking around the squared circle against men hairy as gorillas. Muscular matrons slapping mindless maidens into pinning predicaments. And the midgets, little *putti* mugging in front of the crowd.

"Are you sure that's what you see?"

"I see one person kicking another where she shouldn't. What else am I supposed to see?"

Steel-cage matches and scaffold matches, Indian strap matches and Australian tag-team matches, come-dressed-as-you-are bunkhouse brawls with losers quitting or bleeding, whichever came first—each of them evoking standing ovations from the near-capacity crowd!

"That's what you see with your eye, but there's more to see than that!"

. . . .

"I don't know how much more I can take of this!"

Blatant chokeholds and violent lacerations, Irish whips and Russian sickles, half nelsons and figure-four leg locks, Big Berthas and Good-night Irenes—the children in the Garden were cheering as loudly as their parents!

"But what does it mean?" he shouted. "What does it really mean?"

My question, precisely. At the very least, I put it into their heads—although putting a thought into his head was like rolling a marble around a fishbowl—that what they were seeing had at least one other meaning.

"The thumping and thwacking," he said, "are characteristic of the combatants in a modern American marriage. That was the theme, was it not, of *Who's Afraid of Virginia Woolf?*"

"Not so," she said too seriously, hitting him on the upper arm with her tiny knuckles, "it can't be so."

The wrestlers in the final and climactic match were, I whispered into her ear, Christians of various denominations, striving for superiority in a battle royal, Baptist stomping Lutheran, Anglo Catholic wracking Roman Catholic, Church of Christ chewing up Assembly of God, the winner take all.

. . . .

"See how they love one another," I whispered again, hoping to show her the bankruptcy of the Christian message among its own ministers.

"Stick a fork in him," shouted Fido toward the ring, "he's done!"

Alas, one misstep on the tropological trampoline can lead to a broken leg or a snapped neck, and I must have overstepped my bound. When she asked if the theory I had poured into her ear had any validity, he said he didn't think so and quickly proposed another theory.

In match after match it was good against evil. What's more, though theologians have difficulty recognizing evil even when it's tattooed on their nether cheeks, the motley crowd in Madison Square Garden, half of them literate only in the comic book adventures of super heroes and heroines, had no difficulty at all in recognizing the good guy from the bad guy, the good gal from the bad gal, the good midget from the bad midget. No doubt also their own lives have demonstrated to them over and over again not only the presence of evil in the world but also the constant struggle of good against evil.

There was a compliment in there somewhere for our Infernal Lord, and no doubt my Opposite Number would have been cheered by such grunting

. . . .

and groaning exhibitions if only he had a stomach for the vulgarity and didn't loathe popular culture.

I won't tell you which Christian won the battle royal—he got the final advantage when the referee's back was turned—but I will tell you that the battle went on even after the final bell had sounded.

Augustine in his *Confessions,* if you can remember that maudlin manuscript, described his friend's bloodlust rising at the cutthroat games in the coliseum, resulting in a grisly conversion to the infernal side. I suspected something like that might have happened to my temptand last night. But nothing did happen. They just sat there and shouted back and forth to each other, he liking it rather more than she.

But I got so excited that I left the seat behind them and ran down to the ring where I leaped onto the apron, tore my Brooksweave shirt off, and began pounding flesh, having the time of my life, until I was blindsided by a folding chair at the base of my rented skull. I was dropped to the concrete floor—in the parlance of the wrestling commentator—like a bad habit.

It took me a few minutes to pull myself together and put my attire in order. Aching but feeling refreshed, I was able to accompany the couple out of the Garden, intending to do them more mischief as

. . . .

the evening progressed. The dialogue that follows is —alas—as dreary as they spoke it.

"I don't like football especially," she said, "but I like it better than wrestling. The game has rules, and when the players break the rules, the referee stops the game and steps off a penalty."

"I like wrestling for just the opposite reason. It's unfair, the rules are always broken, and the referee can never right the wrongs. It's more like life."

I will not trouble your last wheezing moments, dear Uncle, with the sort of drivel they drawled after that. Suffice it to say that I draw closer to her with every passing weekend, and not too much time will pass before I close in for the kill.

Yours gladiatorially,

Fleetwood

Most rickety Uncle,

After my escapade last weekend, I have had to spend my week and indeed this weekend in traction, less mobile, I'm afraid, than your frail self. The temptand I was unable to pursue personally, but by virtue of Lavallière I was able to record most of what she said and to reconstruct the rest.

Some time ago I caused her to meet a young Evangelical gentleman who introduced her to the wonderful world of petitionary prayer. He even presented her with a four-color gift catalog—it weighed three pounds—of things she might want to pray for. He also left with her two recently published books on

. . . .

the subject that promised her everything from Rolaids to Rolls-Royces.

I exaggerate, of course, but this young gentlemen also brought her a set of audiotapes promoted by a prosperity preacher whose silvery tongue and golden promises should work for the government and not upon a church's congregation. In the afternoon, when he had left, she read the books and listened to the tapes, making notes and jotting down questions.

That took place during the daylight hours. When night fell, Fido scratched at her door, asking to be let in. Whether he liked it or not, she presided at the range. Having threatened him with a gastronomic gamble like Poached Alligator or Fricasseed Octopus, she finally served Cajun Jambalaya.

Thoroughly bloated from the meal, they stuffed themselves into their outer clothes and went for one of those interminable walks in the cold. Not knowing whether she had been enriched or impoverished by her outing earlier in the day or by the books and tapes later in the day, she brought up the subject of petitionary prayer.

"Do you believe that one gets what one prays for?"

"No."

"Well, what happens to all those prayers that

. . . .

ask for things? Do they go to some sort of dead-letter office?"

"Oh no," he said with some assurance, "they are all answered."

"But you just said . . ."

"God answers them, but only in the way He sees fit."

"You mean to say that if I pray for a horse, I might not get a horse but I might get a giraffe?"

"Yes, metaphorically speaking."

"But then I would have to pray to get rid of the giraffe—you know how low my ceilings are—and He would give me instead a cat, but you know how allergic to cats I am. And so on and so on."

"You make petitionary prayer sound like getting Christmas presents you don't want and trying to return them to the department store without the original receipts."

"That's what *you* make it sound like. No, there's got to be more to it than that."

"Sometimes people get precisely what they pray for, I have no doubt of that, perhaps even a Silver Cloud; but sometimes people don't get what they want, and then they think that God has no ears, or worse, that there is no God."

"How do you know that God hears all those prayers? How do you know that He just hasn't fallen

. . . .

behind in his paperwork? After all, there are four billion people on the earth, and at any one time a fair number of them are praying for things. How can we expect Him to answer them all even if He wanted to, let alone on the same day? I mean, how do I know that He hasn't given my horse to the person who prayed for a giraffe? Does Santa answer all the letters He gets?"

"Does God have a white beard?"

"Questions, questions, questions," she said, hugging his arm as it began to snow. "Do you pray?"

"All the time."

"Do you pray for anything in particular?"

"Not very often."

"Do you pray for me?"

"Now, why would I do a thing like that?"

"Don't you consider me in my unbaptized state a lost soul?"

"Ohhh, you're a lost soul, all right, gamboling away at every chance, but the shepherd is hard on your heels. He'll get you sooner or later if you don't do anything too foolish, and He'll carry you back to the fold. No, I don't pray for you, at least in that way."

"Then in what way?"

"Sometimes I pray that you may have an increase in hilarity."

. . . .

"A what?"

"You're an overly solemn creature, you know, given to introspection and intellection. People of your type psychiatrists have long studied, knowing some of them to explode, and it always seems to happen with a loud pop in a public place. Your only salvation, it seems to me, is hilarity in ever-increasing doses. And hilarity always being in short supply on the world market, I have had to prostrate myself at the divine tribunal to pray for it."

"And has God answered your prayer?"

"Whenever I put this petition before Him, I seem to hear in reply that He will send you no such commodity, that it is scarcer than krypton, that since I have an excess of it, I should be willing to transmit some to you."

"And how did he say this was to be accomplished?"

"From lips to lips," he said, attempting to kiss her in the blizzarding snow.

"You are a totally mystifying man," she said, hitting him repeatedly on the forearm with gloved knuckles. "When am I going to meet your best friend?"

"Would you like to meet him tonight?"

"Woolly's not into wrestling, is he?"

"Not the violent type we saw last weekend, but

. . . .

he's not averse to a tumble on the rug. There's a pay phone. I'll tell him we're coming."

"You mean to say you're going to call a stuffed animal?"

"Let's surprise him instead," he said as he led her down into the subway.

"Is this best friend of yours real, or is he a metaphor? A couple of weeks ago you said he was both."

"Ohhh, he's quite real," he said as they boarded a train, "but I wouldn't want to say that he is without metaphor."

"If this creature had any sanity at all, he should be under the covers and asleep by now."

"On weekdays, yes, but on Saturday nights around nine o'clock he puts on his stocking hat, loops a muffler around his neck, and goes out to buy the Sunday *Times.* Back at the apartment he makes himself a pot of tea—"

"What, no honey?"

"Honeyed to taste, and he sets himself up on the sofa to do the crossword puzzle."

"This I've got to see."

Iron screeching on steel announced their arrival at the Twenty-third Street Station. He led the way a few blocks south and turned into the Coronado,

. . . .

a dismally lit apartment house, a huge homely human presiding at the door.

"It's all I can afford," he said as he unlocked the door to his first-floor apartment.

"Well, where's Woolly?" she asked as she sailed into the narrow living room and looked around.

" 'River through Xanadu,' " said a voice behind her, a voice that was full of velour; "I need a four-letter word that begins with the letter A . . ."

About this time Lavallière's batteries failed—Cadmium has been severely chastised—and so I was unable to record their words. Their actions, however, need little imagination to reconstruct. Next weekend I shall be able to do more than record my temptand's activities, or so I learned from Sprint.

Yours immobilely,

Fleetwood

XXIV

Most exacerbating Uncle,

I have completely succeeded in confusing my temptand when it came to prayer. During the week past, whenever she settled down to pray, she did not know whether to offer the prayer of quiet or the prayer of racket, to ask for something for herself or to meditate on a scriptural passage. By the time she had made up her mind, I was already distracting her with stressful thoughts of office work yet undone that must be done before the following day.

On Saturday morning her Evangelical friend picked her up and took her to the Palm Court, a scone's thrown from the Baptist church on Fifty-sev-

. . . .

enth Street. During breakfast he got up his nerve to ask her if she were a Christian.

Not yet, she said.

He asked her if she knew that the end was nigh, that the final days were near, that Jesus was about to come again.

When she asked how he knew, he said that Evangelical scholars had been able to interpret the prophecies in the Book of Revelation in the light of current events.

And what did they find? she asked.

They found that geopolitical forces were already at work preparing for the final showdown on the plains of Armageddon, with jets and tanks and computer-guided missiles.

Who were guiding the computers in this scenario?

Three characters, a sort of Infernal Trinity, were already hard at work, not precursing the event but pre-cursing it. The hyphen was particularly important, he said, being a copy editor for a monthly magazine of inspiration that enjoyed enormous circulation.

Before Jesus comes again in glory, he promised, there will be a period of great tribulation, marked by apocalyptical sevenses, seals and trumpets

. . . .

and bowls of wrath that will scourge the earth. Operative also will be that Infernal Trinity.

Satan, of course, was necessarily the first person of this trinity, the strong one, the evil one, the prince of this world. Our Infernal Lord will no doubt be pleased when he hears this.

Antichrist was the second person, an attractive fellow with a messiah complex who will lead the Christian community off the straight and narrow path. At our Infernal Lord's request, I have already sent out a casting call and have begun to receive the most amazing résumés and photographs.

False Prophet was the third person, a stooge pretending to be a thaumaturge, whose grand illusion will be to raise Antichrist from the dead. I hope he can do it without mirrors, without passing hoops around the corpse as it rises from the ground. This I plan to televise to the nation and indeed to the world, an illusion more impressive than making the Statue of Liberty disappear.

What about the Whore of Babylon? she asked, a hint of feminism in her voice.

"The clumsy but willing girl from the Levant? Well, she's not one of the Infernal Trinity, if that's what you're hinting at. She's, ahhh well, she's entertainment."

The scenario was all in the Book of Revela-

. . . .

tions with rapture, tribulation, millennium, and judgment.

What was a girl to do? she asked.

She must reform, repent, be born again that she be judged not harshly.

She reminded him that she had not been born once yet let alone twice, at least spiritually. She intended to ask for baptism soon and indeed was shopping around for a denomination. Afraid that she would choose the wrong one and hence be lost forever, he had the temerity to suggest that she would make a good Evangelical.

As on the preceding Saturday, she spent the morning with her Evangelical friend and the afternoon by herself, pondering what he had said. In the evening she talked with Fido.

"Will there be an end?" she asked.

"I think so."

"But when?"

"Anytime between now and then."

"What do you think about the Evangelical scenario?"

"The only question," he answered, "is just how much has been metaphor and how much will be history."

"Does it matter?"

"In both cases the message is the same."

. . . .

"Reform, repent?"

"So it seems."

"But when?"

"For most people the end, such as it is, comes at death, which precedes the endtime scenario, however it's interpreted. Hence, one must reform, repent before the end of one's life."

"When do you think is the best time?"

"Once one has got the message loud and clear, then he or she should act as soon as reasonably possible."

"I am going to act, I have decided that. I am going to be baptized, but what would happen to us if I didn't choose your denomination?"

"We would just go to different churches on Sunday."

"But what if my church attacked your church, saying that it was not the real one, the valid one?"

"Mine, if it knew, would probably counterattack in however civilized a way. But I would not join in the attack. I would be a conscientious objector, knowing that the Holy Spirit was directing your footsteps, as indeed He is directing mine."

"I shall choose soon," she said. "You'll be the second to know."

So much for these poor miserable creatures. She will indeed choose soon. Little does she know,

. . . .

she will choose the Infernal Prince rather than the Supernal Lord, and sirens and whistles will sound and resound throughout the Infernal Region.

Tintinnabulously yours,

Fleetwood

XXV

Most wretched Uncle,

The endtime scenario does have a cinematic quality about it, and it would indeed look good in Technicolor and Panavision. It even has a theme-park quality about it, and I mean that in the best sense. It is preached so often and in such lurid detail that one can imagine it taking place every night of the year as a pyrotechnical display over the lagoon at a Christian end-of-the-world resort.

Mock it though I do, I wouldn't be surprised if it happened just that way. If it does, I shall be able to light a few bonfires myself. The time will be short for us. We will make a few gains, snatch a few notables, rake up some riffraff, but in the end, it will be pain

. . . .

and loss for us in the Infernal World. If I think about it too long, I become paralyzed. Eschatological stress is a terrible thing.

Speaking of pain and loss, I dreamed last night that I was in the middle of a frozen lake, and you know that I have this fear of depths. Well, I truly thought my end had come. There was the deafening sound of a chain saw cutting through ice. I was convinced that once the circle had been completed around me, I would sink to the bottom to tempt no more. I screamed. . . .

"Screaming won't help," said Opposite Number, standing over me, the moon visible over his shoulder. "I have come to warn you that your time is running out. If you have not won your temptand before Easter, then she shall be ours forever, and you will have suffered yet another irretrievable loss." Even in this dream, if dream it were, O.N. sounded sanctimonious. "Why you haven't done it already I really don't know. You've had enough time."

"Will you stop that saw?"

"Could it be that you are losing your touch?"

"I'll match my record against yours anytime."

"I have no intention of putting my record up for scrutiny, superlative though it is." His reply was glacial. "That would be a prideful thing on my part."

The chain stopped whirring, the saw stopped

. . . .

cutting, and I had the strangest sensation of sinking back through the black ice and plummeting down to the depths, yelling and screaming all the while, only bubbles coming from my mouth.

It was then that I awoke and found myself, not at the bottom of the lake or the bottom of my bed, but soaked and shivering in the middle of a skating rink in Central Park. The sun was high; mufflered couples were waltzing to scratchy records. How I got there I have no idea, but when I tried to rise, I fell. I rose again and straggered about on the curved blades that were bolted to highly polished boots. They laughed at me, the snowsuited children who were skittering about the ice with ease.

Next thing I knew, my temptand tripped over me, and I sprawled again, iceburns rising on my cheek. Fido scooped her up, but when he attempted to put me to rights, apologizing all the while, I kicked him in the shin. That sent them on their circular way around the rink, leaving me to avoid being sliced into slivers by the racing and dancing blades of oncoming skaters. Such is my pedestral dexterity, however, that before too many turns I was able to maintain my balance and even increase my speed, cruising within earshot of my temptand and her friend.

"What would you say if I told you that one of the executives, very high up the agency ladder, who

. . . .

prides himself on teaching Sunday school, also has an appetite for pretty young catechizands?"

"I'm not surprised."

"He hires them as though he were stocking his streams with trout."

"It's the same in my office, although the girls aren't so pretty; publishing pays less than advertising."

"If I don't go along with him and his lecherous gang, then it will affect my advancement in the agency."

"Is it possible that you've misread the signals?"

"Of course I've misread the signals. That's why one of the account executives had to put it to me point-blank the other day. What should I do?"

"A couple of things," he said, as the skating switched from clockwise around the rink to anticlockwise. "First of all, if you want to sleep around, then do it, but not because some Harris-Tweeded-dum or Harris-Tweeded-dee pressures you to. Do it because you want to, and do it with someone you like. Second, don't do it even with him. There's this commandment in Genesis. . . ."

"I know the commandments, but it's impossible to observe them all."

"Try we must, and fall we always do, but if

. . . .

we're serious, Jesus forgives and asks us to come back to the fold."

"But if I don't sleep with those bozos at the office or with some of those out-of-town clients who want hands-on experience in the big city, then my career path-tracking will come to a rude halt, and I'll spend the rest of my days, writing commercials for Ti-D-bol."

"So what?" asked the young man with the insouciance of one who's professional life was not at stake. "With regard to the commandments, it's better to have tried and failed, than not to have tried at all."

"Did you pluck that one from the Book of Proverbs?"

So much for this icy little escapade. They skated on and on to the throbbing melodies. Unable to switch directions on the rink without severe vertigo, I had to turn in my rented skates and nurse my whirling head with hot chocolate. I shall tempt them both to bed, but next weekend, when my warmth has returned and the swelling in my lower joints has receded. Fornication will fissure his faith, have no doubt about that, and it will muddle her faith before she has a chance to fire it in the kiln.

Yours wobblingly,

Fleetwood

XXVI

Most despicable Uncle,

That I should put my temptand to the triathlonic test I knew you would eventually suggest. But I want you to know that I haven't done it in decades. I am doing it now only to prove your wrong-headedness on yet another front.

Although not obliged denominationally to do so, she has undertaken an elaborate program of Lenten fasting, which began some weeks ago and will conclude at midnight on Easter Sunday. Hence, in her weakened state I put the triathlon to her.

Wednesday, she intended to eat nothing and drink only water. At every turn as she toddled around

. . . .

Manhattan, I confronted her with bakeries and arrested her with aromas: brioche and croissant, English muffins and Irish soda bread, Jewish rye and German pumpernickel. At every turn she salivated, but she swallowed the water and held on until midnight. So much for the first temptation in the triathlon.

On Friday, when she was lunching at the top of the Empire State Building, I encouraged her to think that if she really believed what she prayed, she would throw herself off and before hitting the pavement a hundred floors below, she would be caught by the outstretched arms of the Supernal Lord. She found the thought confusing at first, and when I proceeded to demonstrate, running for the balustrade with a view to vaulting over it, I came into smart contact with a pane of Plexiglas. To prevent suicides, it seems, the building security had erected this see-through barrier to prevent despairing souls from taking off into the open air. I tried to explain what I was doing to the guard, but he wouldn't listen. He merely hustled me into the stairwell and told me not to stop until I had reached the street below. So much for the second temptation in the triathlon.

On Saturday last, I led the way to the World Trade Center, took the whooshing elevator to the hundredth floor. When the doors opened, she glided to-

. . . .

ward the floor-to-ceiling windows and began pointing out one site after another. Fido, however, a sudden wave of acrophobia overwhelming his psyche, remained pinned to the wall. I took these few moments so fortuitously offered to approach the window and suggest to the temptand that all of what she saw—it was a clear day and she could see all the way to the curvature of the earth—could be hers if she would only sleep with her cohorts and consort with them in other activities unconducive to belief in the Supernal Lord.

Hoboken would be nice, I thought I heard her say. The rest of New Jersey she didn't want, and she wasn't sure about the boroughs of Queens and Brooklyn, but there were certain sections of Manhattan that interested her greatly. Before I could tell her that I couldn't break up the lot, that she would have to take them all or nothing, she realized that the person by her side was not her friend. She ran back to the wall, where he remained as if centripetally pinned, and helped him to the elevator, where she put his hand into a five-year-old's, who promised to take good care of the sick adult. As the doors closed, she said she would see him in the lobby; she just had to get a few things from the gift shop. So much for the third temptation in the triathlon.

You would consider my activities a failure, and

. . . .

indeed I have not yet succeeded. But this is a gutsy girl; the more she resists, the more I desire her for my Infernal Kingdom. What has failed is the triathlon itself. It didn't work in the first century, and it doesn't work now. Even at *Schola Temptorum* when you explained it to us, we thought it antique.

Thanks to Lavallière I was able to monitor the couple's rambling conversations for the rest of the day, a summary of the important points of which follows. May I remind you that it is from these thousands of seemingly inconsequential conversational and behavioral moments that I discern patterns and derive courses of action.

He proposed marriage to her for the hundredth time, and for the hundredth time she put him off.

It was not that she didn't love him; it was that she had to decide about God first.

He didn't mind waiting, so long as he was second in line.

She was beginning a course of instruction that would take her through Lent and culminate, she hoped, with baptism on Easter Sunday.

When he asked her again what denomination she favored, she declined to say, whispering only that she wanted to do this without him so that forever

. . . .

after she could clearly state that he had not influenced her decision.

Could he ask her on Easter Monday? he wanted to know.

What games people play!

Back at his apartment on Saturday night, he cooked dinner for her, a virtuoso performance with an oven of uncertain temperature. From that oven with grease-specked window, Woolly took the bubbling Pyrex and put it on a trivet. "He doesn't need mitts," her friend said even before she asked.

"Salmon casserole," she said, not wanting to taste it. "My favorite."

Woolly said he would pour the wine if someone would pop the cork from the neck of the bottle. Around nine o'clock he went out for the Sunday *Times.*

"Do you believe in an afterlife?"

"I don't *know* there's an afterlife, but I *believe* there's an afterlife."

"Will it be like the classical underworld? Will it be a renaissance utopia? Will it be a science fiction overworld?"

"It'll be one of adoration, souls huddled like angels before the Lord, their wings folded about them."

"Sounds like the Book of Revelation again."

. . . .

"It's more like a metaphor than anything else," he said, passing a dessert plate to her. "Would you care for a cream puff?"

"Do you know how many tens of thousands of calories there are in these things?" she asked as she helped herself to the plumpest of them. "Will there be any socializing? I mean, will I see my mother and father there, and will they see me?

"I suppose so."

"But how do you know this?"

"It's in the New Testament."

"But don't the demythologizers whack away at the passages that talk about Heaven?"

"I'd have to say that if I know anything at all about Heaven, I've come by it, not in a methodological way, but in a mystical way."

"Now you're going to tell me you're a mystic?"

"Anyone who prays regularly may be called a mystic, and what I believe about Heaven, I have come by through reading the New Testament and praying over it."

Steam whistled through the iron radiators as the temperature outside the Coronado dropped.

"What about Woolly? Will he qualify for the afterlife?"

"If he behaves himself, and there's no reason

. . . .

to think he won't; after all, his is an unfallen species."

Desire steamed through their veins and arteries. They embraced, and the amatory adventure once begun would have continued if they hadn't heard a nervous cough.

"That will be Oliver," he said, pointing to a Pinocchio-like puppet sitting on the baker's-rack bookcase, whose cheeks had blotches like Red Delicious. "May I present my good friend Oliver M. Sudden?"

"What does the M stand for?"

"Maple."

At this point I turned off my playback device. There is only so much sludge a person can take in any one twenty-four-hour period. Have no fear! I shall encoil them both in their own bedsprings.

Carcinoma tells me that bellows have been prescribed, once every four hours, to fan your ebbing flame. I do hope to present you with one last present before you flicker your last.

Yours relentlessly,

Fleetwood

Most malicious Uncle,

It was Palm Sunday, as some denominations called it, the week before Easter Sunday, a good day to surrender if you are a Southerner, for on that April day in 1865 Grant accepted the surrender of Lee, thus ending the war between the Northern and Southern states.

For the last few weeks she had fought hard against the onslaughts of the Supernal Lord. Now she was tired and could fight no longer. She was outnumbered and outmaneuvered. Suicide was always a possibility, if only to be entertained and then rejected. She could wait for death the next time the Enemy

. . . .

charged. The only other course of action was surrender.

It would be hard to surrender with dignity, she thought as she snipped the buttons from her uniform, especially when she knew that the terms would be unconditional. There was some consolation at least in the thought that the Enemy did indeed take prisoners. She hauled down the stars and bars and knelt in prayer, waiting for the inevitable.

She did not have long to wait. She heard horses outside, boots with spurs on the stairway, a knock on the door. He stepped in and saluted. She offered her sword; he accepted it. She expected him to snap the blade in two; instead he returned it to her ceremoniously. She thought she would have to give up her sidearms, her property, but she was allowed to keep them; she would need them all in the first months ahead as a Christian. The formal ceremony, with papers to sign, would take place next Sunday, he said, and he would see her there. But what about the snipped buttons, symbols of defeat? She was supposed to hand them over, but he closed her fingers around them. Tiddlywinks, he suggested. He shook hands with her and was gone.

Somewhere in the neighborhood voices were raised, singing "Auld Lang Syne." She was quiet, very quiet, and she mused, before drifting off to

. . . .

sleep, how much things were the same and how much they would change.

I tell you this, dear Uncle, because it has all the notes of weekday melodrama about it. Have no fear. I am writing the script for the coming week, and I shall throw some surprises, some antipersonnel devices if I have to, in her path. She will never make it alive to next Sunday.

Yours subversively,

Fleetwood

Most deleterious Uncle,

As Good Friday dawned, my temptand became more and more preoccupied with what, if anything, happened after the death of the son of man or the son of God or whoever He was in the New Testament. Over and over again she has read the resurrection narratives. Who rolled away the stone? she wanted to know, and where was the body? The Evangelists did not satisfy her on this point, nor did the biblical theologians who have pored over the phenomenon for the last nineteen hundred years.

Prayer ofter revealed the answers to the speculative questions of theology, Fido was fond of spouting, and prayer she had already found was a conve-

. . . .

nient mode of transport back into biblical times. Hence she conveyed herself this time to Jerusalem. There she found the garden of Gethsemane and asked the gardener, who was propagating plants, cutting and budding and grafting, if he knew the whereabouts of a certain tomb. Muttering to himself something unflattering about the sort of tourists who were tearing up his spiritual garden, he motioned to the far end where there was a cave, to the left of which was a stone large enough to secure the opening.

She entered the cave, not in the spirit of a grand spelunker but rather mousily, and found some sepulchral linens. Turning, she saw the risen Lord, perhaps a person, perhaps an afterimage of a dear friend who had died. She did not reject the image, nor did she reach out to touch it. She merely gazed at it and believed that Jesus was Lord, that He was no longer here, that He had risen from the dead as He had promised, and that He was roaming about, seeking whom He might embrace.

That she might appreciate the tomb experience the more, I rolled the stone against the opening, entrapping her inside. Surprised, she called for help a few times and then sat down, expecting that the gardener would soon discover her, let her out, and disabuse her of her resurrectional thoughts.

Like Miss Marple or Harriet Vane, she went

. . . .

over and over the facts of the case and the theories about what it meant. Death and resurrection were the essential components of all the theories of atonement.

One such theory held that Jesus was not divine and indeed did not rise, but that he was a good man, a moral man, and the very model of human existence. This theory, she thought, smacked of the classroom; it had no street value because it was the very theory used by those who did not believe in the divinity of Jesus, who felt that He was first cousin to Buddha and Mohammed.

Another theory had God the Father negotiating with our Infernal Lord, trying to buy back mankind from original sin; it was remarkably accurate as far as it went. Indeed, it was not far in feeling from marketing the considerable redemptive merits, if any, of that crazy crucifixion like stamps redeemable at supermarkets. For a certain number of such stamps, one could obtain all sorts of spiritual favors.

I could always invent my own theory of atonement, she thought to herself as the gardener didn't come and claustrophobia began to crawl on little legs all over her body. She screamed. At this moment I swept her from the tomb in the outskirts of Jerusalem to the morgue in the heart of New York City, where I opened one refrigerated compartment after another and peeled away the plastic shrouds to prove to her

. . . .

that dead was dead and that somewhere back in Jerusalem there had to be a body with a tag on the big toe, reading *Jesus of Nazareth, King of the Jews.*

She screamed again. I left her apartment, hearing her screams of pain and delusion, and knew that she would continue through the night. I knew also that she would not recover from the cadaverous vision I had just given to her and that she would never take that final, fatal step toward baptism. Indeed, I felt she would not ever again even dip a tentative toe into the Jordan.

Formaldehydeously yours,

Fleetwood

Most feeble Uncle,

"If I'm so happy, then why am I so sad?" she asked Fido over dinner in her apartment on Holy Saturday night. She had burned the rice and scorched the brussels sprouts and demonstrated an unleakable shaker which sprayed orange juice all over the room whenever it was jounced with vigor. She was in a miserable mood.

"If this is sad, then I would hate to see you mad!"

The verbal fight continued and generated into a physical one, with her hurling pillows and him tossing them back. She showed him the door several

. . . .

times and literally had to shove him out and lock and bolt it so that she could dissolve into tears in private.

She was exhausted, too tired to read, but she did try to pray. During this quiet time I gave her a choice, either to drop off into sleep or to envision what would come if she persisted in this crazy course of action that would climax in baptism on Sunday. Her family would renounce her, her friends would revile her. Every structure that she had known since childhood would be destroyed and every relationship she had as an adult would collapse.

Without too much effort on my part, she began to see herself in rags, her body scraped, her feet blistered, limping through her devastated life as though she were stepping through the rubble of a bombed-out Berlin or a burned-out Hiroshima. There was nothing left of her personal possessions. There was not even the family dog yipping and yapping about the smoldering ruins. Wondering why she had done all this and whether there was indeed anything to look forward to, she sat down on a wheelbarrow, which had somehow survived the devastation. She needed only a Magnum photographer to immortalize the distant, unfocused look of a convertend confronting that inevitable stage in every conversion pro cess, wreckage. Stronger persons than she have crumbled at the sight.

. . . .

Almost in despair, she called her green-corduroy friend and asked if anything like this had ever happened to him. She expected the answer no because he was a cradle Christian. He countered, using the oldest ploy in the book, that what appeared to be cruel and unusual punishment was in reality par for the course for a convert. What appeared to be destruction today was no dream; it was real, all right; but tomorrow, he said, quoting a work she herself had often quoted, *Gone With the Wind,* was another day; reconstruction would begin tomorrow, and who knew what new edifices and relationships would be built on the same site.

He asked her if she had chosen a denomination yet. She said she had. When he asked which it was, she refused to tell, saying only that she would meet him tomorrow for brunch, around noon at Rockefeller Plaza. When he said that he wanted to go to church with her to witness the baptism, she declined, saying for the hundredth time that she wanted to go through this all by herself. When he said that he would be waiting on her doorstep at dawn, she laughed and said she would leave by the back door.

Unfortunately for me, she took some comfort in his words before I was able to deaden her phone. Needless to say, as time ran out, I continued that bombed-out feeling in my temptand. She smelled it

. . . .

and tasted it, and she thought it. Before her head hit the pillow, the telephone rang two times. Her parents called to inform her that she was making the mistake of her life. Her grandparents dialed long-distance to say that they would suffer seizures if she converted to Christianity. One of her co-workers, who lived in the same block and dropped in unexpectedly, said, when she heard what my temptand planned to do on the morrow, that she was selling her soul into spiritual bondage.

In the few hours that I have left, the temptand will relent. She has turned out to be a stronger-willed person than I had expected, but I shall break her one way or the other.

Yours perspiringly,

Fleetwood

XXX

Most moribund Uncle,

This is the last letter I shall write to Dimchurch, Carcinoma having informed me of your passing; you coughed a couple of times, she said, a few wisps as if from a snuffed wick, and you were gone. Hence this letter, with perhaps too-detailed a re-creation of the events of the last twenty-four hours, is meant really for the archives.

From the first day I was introduced to her, the temptand had proceeded, occasionally daunted but daring enough to push on, toward baptism on Easter Sunday morning. All of my temptorial arts had failed within, of course, the unfair time restraints imposed on me from above . . . or seemed to have failed. I

. . . .

had taken the precaution of appropriating a taxicab the night before; I ran it through a car wash, had the interior vacuumed, and inserted my photograph in the hack bureau license. Around midnight I pulled up in front of her brownstone apartment and parked, wanting to be sure not to miss her departure for church in the morning. Who knew, she might even attempt a sunrise service, although sporting money would put her down for the noontime liturgy.

No—I answer to the question that our archivist will surely ask—I had no intention of driving her to that accursed event. Anyone familiar with organized crime in America would know that what I planned to do was to follow her and run her down even as she crossed the street to enter the church; a professional hit, police investigators would certainly conclude, her valuables still intact.

I must have dozed off because the next thing I remember was a handkerchief pressed to my nose. When I promised to behave, the handkerchief, which had been dampened with some dizzying spirits, was removed. Not blinfolded, I found myself sitting in the backseat of what appeared to be a very long limousine—the diesel fumes were unmistakable—flanked by two hulking creatures who just had to be emissaries from the Supernal Lord.

At Central Park I was unloaded rather too

. . . .

quickly from the limo and fell. The goons picked me up and hustled me into the park. It was still dark when I was shoved onto the Bridge of Sighs and motioned to cross to the other side. I did not like the looks of this, but I was clearly outnumbered.

"Surely you'll want a sprig of dogwood on this holy day," said Opposite Number, who was waiting for me in the middle of the bridge.

"Damn the dogwood!" I said, flinging it over the side.

"You've never really appreciated the beauty of this world."

"What is the meaning of this?"

"I'm taking back the temptand I entrusted to you."

"But you can't take her from me! Not just when I am about to succeed."

"You've had more than enough time."

"But that would not be fair!"

"Who are you to talk of fair?"

"You said I had until Easter Sunday."

"The sun is rising, even as we argue. Our darling young temptand—"

"Our?"

"When you were tempting her to the left, I was at her other side, tempting her to the right."

. . . .

"I must protest in the strongest possible terms!"

"As I was saying, she is already up and dressing. . . ."

"But this is in direct violation of the Orderly Departure Program!"

"Soon she'll be on her way to church. . . ."

"You're not listening to me, are you?"

"Soon she'll feel the healing waters of baptism."

"You want me to beg, don't you? That's why you've dragged me here. You want a little late-night entertainment. You want me to get down on my knees and beg for more time. Well, I won't beg!"

"You don't have to beg. We intend to give you another chance."

"Another chance to fail, you mean. Who is it this time?"

"Her friend."

"Not the one in the green corduroy jacket?"

"None other. He's gotten a little too big for his britches, we feel; he's outgrown everything Barney's has to offer."

"Please, not him!"

"A good stretch of temptation will bring him down a peg or two."

"Anybody but him!"

. . . .

"That sounds ungrateful."

"What I mean to say is, if you don't want him in *your* place, I certainly don't want him in *mine.* Please look around. There has to be some limbo you can stash him in."

"What have you got against him? He seems a nice-enough fellow."

"Too marshmallowy for my taste. He'll toast on the outside, but on the inside he'll remain all white and runny."

"Really," said Opposite Number with a note of finality, stapling a sprig on my lapel, "you should sport some dogwood on this glorious day."

With the sun rising over the East River, roseate rays creeping like fingers between the tall buildings, I was blinded for a moment. Then I realized that I was alone on the bridge. Running out of the park and down to the Fifties, I raced eastward toward the river. There was a slim chance that I had been dreaming all this. The taxicab that I had purloined was still there. I got into the driver's seat just as she appeared at the top of the steps of her brownstone. New clothes she was wearing; her dress was blue, her gloves were white, her handbag was black, and her hat was a crazy little pillbox the color of her dress.

Perhaps I had dreamed the episode in the park. I went to turn the key, only to realize that I no

. . . .

longer had it. Wouldn't you know, the herald angels had turned my pockets inside out during the struggle. I hotwired the ignition and got the taxi running, but just as I pressed the accelerator to the floor, the wheel responded flaccidly; as she passed in front of me, the cab wobbled to a halt. I got out to examine the tires: all four were flat, someone having nipped the valves with a razor.

"Good morning," she said, thinking I had stopped out of courtesy. "I like the dogwood in your lapel."

Unthinkable blasphemies I shouted in response and reached in the window to press the horn. At least that worked, and loudly too. She just turned and flashed me an Eastery smile.

I close this letter and indeed this correspondence with some sadness, having failed—albeit momentarily—to snare this gutsy young creature for the Infernal Kingdom. But there will be other times, other places. Another sadness comes with the knowledge of your death, knowing that I am the next generation to die. With however much time I have left, I vow to pursue with unceasing diligence whomever I can find for the Infernal Kingdom and my Infernal Lord.

Just then, someone got into the cab—I saw a flash of green and heard the rub of one wale of cordu-

. . . .

roy against another—and handed me a hundred-dollar bill.

"Follow that girl and step on it!" he demanded in a voice I knew only too well. "We're late for church."

"What church?"

"You know," he said tentatively, "I don't really know."

Flicking the ON DUTY sign off, I threw him out of the cab forever!

And so this dreary correspondence comes to an end.

Totally deflated,

Fleetwood

www.ingramcontent.com/pod-product-compliance
Lightning Source LLC
LaVergne TN
LVHW050647100826
845148LV00011B/2025

* 9 7 8 1 5 5 6 3 5 8 0 0 5 *